Drawings by Olin Dows (1904 – 1981)

CROOK'S PARA DISE

DAVID MANDY

PREFACE

It doesn't hurt to remind you that this is a work of fiction based on fairly accurate history. The similarities to real people and places are coincidental. The historical houses of Crum Elbow take on a life of their own in the story. One of my great inspirations for this book was Olin Dows. Dows's enchanting pencil drawings from his book *Franklin Roosevelt at Hyde Park* provide a sublime window into the visual history before the onset of suburban sprawl. The soulfulness of FDR's fireside chats came in part from the dignity of this rural community. He addressed his neighbors because he believed that global and national issues could be transacted and resolved locally. Surely, the voice of Valentine Hitch is a modern-day fireside chat.

For my parents

CHAPTER 1

For generations, the river families had been the eyes and the ears of the land. They were rooted to the soil and thought about future generations. They certainly felt a spiritual connection with this historic landscape. But then the dreaming stopped.

—Valentine Hitch, *Crook's Paradise*

It was another cloudless day in Los Angeles: sunny and perfect. Every day there was sunny and perfect, but that sameness had a tendency to blur the weeks into months and years—twenty years for Philip Livingston Hitch. It was hard to believe that it was the early fall of 2001, just days before everything changed. Known as Livingston until he moved west, he shed his blue blazer and became Livy; at six-three, he towered over everyone. His long reddish-brown hair showed no signs of graying anytime soon. He was known to wear lace-up hiking boots, even with shorts on the hottest of days. He looked like a misplaced mountain man, like he was trapped in the younger Jeff Bridges's body. He was on his way to Studio City to lay down tracks for a Coca-Cola commercial.

It had been Livy's good fortune to meet voiceover agent Bud Nathanson at a party. Bud gushed over Livy's great radio voice. At that moment, he gave him his card and a job for life. Livy now had one of the most recognizable voices in America. He had worked on all the iconic brands: Coca-Cola, Maxwell House, and Apple. He had money, flexibility, and freedom, along with some curious blinders. His past remained unprocessed, frozen in time.

The lingering smell of smoke and sunbaked rubber was in the air. Pile-ups on I-5 were nothing unusual—but going on three hours to travel fifteen miles was a first for Livy. He got back in his car to protect himself from the sun and chugged a bottle of water. Thankful he'd grabbed his mail on the way out, he started sorting through the mess, which had been scattered in the accident. After separating out his royalty checks, one letter caught his attention. The Spenserian script in the style of the Coca-Cola logo was a giveaway. The address on the back of the envelope confirmed it: Valentine Winthrop Hitch, Burleighwood, Crum Elbow on the Hudson.

Livy's Uncle Valentine still preferred writing letters rather than picking up the phone and, even less, sending ghastly electronic mail. His uncle's letter was brief. Valentine assured Livy that he wasn't dead yet but had a few important decisions to make about the family's ancestral home on the Hudson. Livy dreaded any conversation about the fate of Burleighwood. When he moved to California, he still couldn't separate the scene of his happiest childhood memories from pain. It was all pain. Livy leaned his head back and thought about the end of his junior year at Princeton, the year he had made the momentous decision to not come back. He was done pleasing his father. His dear old dad had departed from the family, leaving his mother for a young nubile. His mom's response? To drown in her bathtub after a pleasant painkiller evening.

The official story was that she died in her sleep. Livy knew he had been wisely selfish in leaving his family. But it was too difficult there to avoid the memory and perhaps the guilt of his mother's death.

Livy had expected Valentine to push back on his decision to drop out of college. But he'd met no resistance. He could remember his uncle's warm, understanding baritone.

*   *   *

"Aside from the obvious, how are you doing, Livingston?" his uncle asked, steering his 1937 Pierce-Arrow convertible sedan with long black-side-winding fenders shining in the sun.

"I've never felt so free in my life."

"You've become un-Hitched. Good for you."

"I feel unhinged. I'm going to California."

"That's where you probably should be. Since the Gold Rush, people have been going to California in quest of a shining future. By the time you hit the Pacific, there is nowhere left to go. It's our version of the Promised Land. The East is caught up in its own gravity."

"I like that. That's where I'm going—to the Promised Land to get some of that California transpersonal boost I've been reading about."

"You're a brave soul, Livingston. Not everyone is so bold. I'm going to miss you, but it's time to fly. It's time for you to draft your own Declaration of Independence."

CHAPTER 2

Postwar concrete sealed the fate of the Roosevelt era. It was the end of fieldstone demarcations, and the onset of mass cookie cutting.

—Valentine Hitch, *Crook's Paradise*

Valentine Hitch, at the wheel of his vintage touring car, a projection of his *Chitty Chitty Bang Bang* elegance, followed the Johnny Appleseed Highway north, past the explosion of red, white, and blue patriotism. Eight months later, the impact of 9/11 was still being felt collectively along the Hudson River at Crum Elbow. People were searching for truth. He knew he had only so much time before the trauma wore off and complacency returned. Since his days as *Life Magazine*'s ace photographer covering segregation in the south during the fifties, Valentine had been compiling photographs documenting the depth of crookery in his own backyard. Valentine's camera had become a time machine, roller-coasting between the decades and the centuries. The way he saw it, the town's planners had squandered Crum Elbow for a quick buck. Crum Elbow was now run by the Grubbs. Every year, thousands of tourists came to visit Franklin Roosevelt's birthplace expecting to find Norman Rockwell. Instead, they found a scene out of Norman Mailer.

Valentine's first stop was at the recently bulldozed and staked-out lot across from the tourist entrance to the home of Franklin D. Roosevelt affectionately named Springwood by FDR's mother. It was late spring in the Hudson Valley and the cherry blossoms had made their statement and fallen. A man wearing a foreman's white safety helmet called out to him, "Hey, nice ride buddy, you need help?"

"I was just wondering what part of Disneyland this might be?" Valentine asked, cocking his head back Roosevelt-style.

"You're in the wrong county for that. This is Grubb country," the man said, walking over.

Valentine could feel the chemicals in his brain mutating. Just the idea of the Grubb family triggered disgust. The Grubbs had been messing with Crum Elbow for three generations. Grandpa Grubb subdivided Americana into low-cost housing developments. His namesake, Homer Junior, then proceeded to bulldoze the mile-long stand of ancient sycamore trees along Route 9 and redecorate it with strip malls, parking lots, and gas stations. By the end of the second wave, Grubb Jr. had completely blocked the view of the river from the old Post Road. Now the third generation, Homer Grubb 3.0, was busy expanding mall-to-mall carpeting along the river.

The foreman leaned into the car. "Between you and me, buddy, the Grubbs do things a little differently than old school."

"How so?" Valentine asked, intrigued.

"After Homer Junior took title to this land, he peed on all four corners to mark his territory."

"Coyote protection?"

"Nope, family tradition. Started with Homer's father."

Valentine hesitated for a moment. "Ah, the revenge of the underdogs. I imagine the previous generations of Grubbs were more peed upon than doing the peeing. Do you think Homer Junior would mind if I take a picture of the meadow before they dig it up and build some hideous structure?"

"Junior couldn't care less. He's flipping the land to the Chicken Charlie franchise. You just missed our new boss man, Rupert Obermeyer. Nice guy. He asked us to call him Obie. He likes to take care of his neighbors. So, go ahead, fire away."

The foreman tipped his white helmet and went about his business. Valentine was sporting a wilderness photographer's khaki pants, Nike Air Jordan high-tops, and a red bandanna tied around his neck. He picked up his Leica 35-millimeter camera and rose from the car seat with a jingle from the loose film canisters in his photo vest. He owned many vests.

Today, it was the black-and-white one.

Valentine took a flurry of pictures of the unspoiled landscape from different angles. He'd been fighting these developers since what seemed like the dawn of time, certainly since the 1950s. Their wildfire culture was burning as out of control as fast-food grease. Two hundred years of slow-moving river time had lost its triple-A rating, sidelined by a fast-moving Chicken Charlie burger.

Once snuggled back into the seat behind the classic wooden hulahoop-sized steering wheel with its well-worn silver horn, Valentine fired up the straight eight and headed another 200 yards down the highway. He parked in an empty movie theater lot, which lay directly across the street from the original entrance to the Roosevelt family place. Out of his whole family, he was the only person who admired FDR.

The brownstone gate posts had been padlocked since 1945, when FDR's blue Ford Phaeton convertible had been parked for eternity in the basement of the presidential library. Feeling a little crankier and less flexible than he used to be, Valentine had resorted to using his tartan golf bag from the sixties as a dolly to wheel his tripods and other tools of his trade. It got heavier and heavier every year. Valentine got out of the Pierce-Arrow, pulled his "studio on wheels" out of the backseat, and in the absence of oncoming cars, crossed Route 9 with golf bag in tow. Negotiating a drainage ditch, he grabbed the bag and lifted it over the low stone wall. Gingerly straddling the wall to the other side, he proceeded down a quarter of a mile of graveled road flanked by a double row of maple trees.

Now, with his body in rapid physical decline and feeling a little sorry for himself, Valentine envied Roosevelt's grit, paralyzed from the waist down at thirty-nine years of age, totally determined to walk with crutches from his house to the Post Road and back.

Although he never got as far as the road, FDR did make it to the White House.

Valentine continued through the shadows of the maple trees to the front lawn. Minutes into the lush grass, he stood for a moment at the spot overlooking the turn in the Hudson River where Winston Churchill had been captured meditating at his easel, paintbrush in hand during the early war years. There were certain landscapes where the American spirit had taken root. Places where the light seemed to shine brighter, where rivers sang. To Valentine, Crum Elbow was such a place. This mysterious spot, which 17th century English explorer Henry Hudson dubbed "the crooked elbow," was spilling over with creative genius in the pivotal years of our nation's history. This turn in the river indeed marked turning points. It breathed revolutionary fire and sacred geometries into the American rebellion. It inspired a steamboat and a thousand paintings that captured the color and depth of the light. And it was at Crum Elbow where Franklin Roosevelt drew his inspiration, found his legs again, and defeated Hitler.

Over two hundred years ago, the original Crook, Charles Crook, had created a paradise at Crum Elbow for his son, who'd lost his eyesight in a hunting accident. Valentine set up his tripod on the high escarpment overlooking the river valley. His long telephoto lens served as his binoculars. He focused in on a burial-ground encircled by gravestones, all that remained of the Crook family. Generations of winter storms and geological time had moved the stones into funny angles and cleansed these markers of any trace of identity.

This dilapidated gravesite was where the park rangers would periodically take their smoking break, maintaining a kind of oral tradition.

When Valentine returned to the movie theater lot, Kingdom of Heaven Towing was flat-bedding his beloved touring car. More crooks!

Valentine dashed over. "Please, that's my car."

"It's nice, friend, but you're illegally parked. This is movie-theater property. The movies don't start until seven."

"No crime being early."

"This car sure is a beauty. Got any ID?"

Valentine dug into his wallet, pulled out two fifty-dollar bills and handed them to the man, who then examined U.S. Grant closely. "Yes, I see the resemblance. Let me give you your car back," the tow truck driver said.

Before returning home from crook hunting, Valentine made a quick stop to check his mail. He pushed open the wooden swinging doors of the post office and glided past his friend Olin Dows's mural of his ancestors— helpful folks putting out fires and doing good deeds for their brethren. It was hard to find those kinds of citizens anymore. Crum Elbow had lost its congregation. The straight-thinking, public-spirited people who had held it all together were either dead or scattered like milkweed. Crum Elbow had become part of an endless, franchise-ridden highway sprawling down to Tarrytown. Where had all the good people gone?

Valentine spun the combination lock of the family's long-held brass and glass postal box. He discovered letters that had been resting there for days. There were several from the assessor's office. No great surprise. After his mother died in 1981, Valentine bought out his siblings' shares of Burleighwood, which meant he never had enough money to properly care for the place, much less pay the taxes on time. The royalties covered his basics but could not keep up with the taxes. "I need a miracle. I need a batch, a whole batch of them," he muttered and tucked the letters in his breast pocket.

Burleighwood was one of three historic Hudson River estates at Crum Elbow. Tucked between the Rogers and Roosevelt country places, Burleighwood had been built on water-lot number six of the

Great Nine Partners Patent. The earliest part of the main house had been completed in 1762.

Coming through the ivy gates, instead of slowing down, Valentine accelerated past a fading sign: CHILDREN GO SLOWLY. He scanned the vast rolling vista of abandoned fields and withered apple orchards off to the right. Toward the river and through the woods, he approached his residence looming against the blue horizon. From there, he could see the railroad bridge spanning the tidal river. Burleighwood had begun as "two rooms on the river" with the kitchen in the basement. The original structure had been enlarged with wings added to the north and south during the late nineteenth century. The Hitch family home had held the center of American life since its founding, including for a certain spell of time when it had been an extension of the Underground Railroad. Burleighwood seemingly had countless rooms, dozens of fireplaces, and over two hundred windows. Just having the windows cleaned proved bankrupting. Every time Valentine crossed the threshold, he was confronted by the portraits of strong, independent men and women reaching back to the birth of America. The Hitches and their tribe of Astors, Roosevelts, and Delanos were part of the Empire State Ascendency in the Gilded Age. Valentine was on a first-name basis, not only with the crowd illuminated by picture lights in the entrance hall, but also with the lesser celebrated, twentieth-century Hitches relegated to dimmer corridors.

CHAPTER 3

My great-grandfather, who stole the sun, told his son, who told me.

—Valentine Hitch, *Crook's Paradise*

Jessie Chandler, ten-year resident of New York City, had the trip from her apartment on Ninety-Third Street between Madison and Fifth Avenues to her office on Seventy-Second Street and York Avenue timed to the minute. She knew that if she left by 8:10 a.m., she'd be guaranteed to get to work on time. Anything after that, she was at the mercy of larger forces. On this particular morning, she was found running down the street in her Reeboks, trying to hail a taxi at quarter of nine, her long auburn hair still wet from the shower. After several attempts to catch a cab, she slowed to a fast walk headed down Fifth Avenue. Then she heard a melodious voice.

"Madame, how is this beautiful day today doing for you?" someone asked with a delightful lilt. Jessie looked over to her right and the God of the Distressed had taken the form of a grinning Bengali cab driver. "Get in. Get in. It's very clear to me, Madame. I can see that you're in some kind of hurry." He charmed Jessie right into his cab and off they went down Fifth.

There was something different about this particular day. She could feel it like a change in the weather.

"Madame, what kind of day are you doing?"

"You're way too happy. What planet are you from?"

"Very far away, Madame."

At 9:15 a.m., Jessie barreled through the doors of Sotheby's, wearing a short, black skirt, soft, gray cashmere sweater, and her signature green beret. She exited on the third floor and headed for her cubicle, which was stacked with moving boxes. Instead of moving up the company ladder, she was thinking of the chairlift to the top of Sun Valley.

Her desk was piled high with slides and catalogs that she had been transferring to boxes. She reached into the bottom drawer and pulled out a stack of photographs. The top one was the picture taken back when her life had been fully booked with cocktail parties, charity events, art auctions, and dinner parties. She took a closer look at the woman made-up like a peacock standing next to her ex, who had looked so good on paper, now done and gone. Jessie fired the photograph like a coin into the trash. She turned to the last remaining picture on the bulletin board of her much younger self with no makeup, triumphant in overalls. Her farmer-self under a tack. She could feel her fresh air girl coming up for air. This part of her had never left. She had been climbing the status apparatus for nearly a decade but its seductive spell had worn off.

Suddenly the auction house's lead bloodhound, Gordon Hall, poked his nose into her five-by-five, exposed-ceiling "office."

"Good morning, Jessie. I know you're half out of here, but I have one more *Mission: Impossible* for you."

"What's up?"

"Have you ever heard of Valentine Hitch?"

"The photographer?"

"The one and only. Every time Mr. Hitch needs money, we receive a call. Usually, Valentine comes up with some valuable art to sell."

"I'm not surprised. He sure has the eye."

"We've auctioned some of the Hitch family paintings in the past. They had one of the largest collections of Sargent in America. John Singer Sargent courted Valentine's grandmother."

"I can see you want me to meet Valentine?"

"That's the mission. Who knows what you'll find up there? He'll meet you at the Rhinecliff train station."

"Sure, why not!"

Jessie packed her belongings for the day trip and caught a cab across town to Penn Station. Jessie walked briskly past soldiers in camouflage holding M-16s in their hands posted at every entrance. All she could really deal with was finding Gate 32, and boarding the Amtrak Express train to Rhinecliff.

Ten minutes later, her train emerged from the dark tunnel into the light. It rolled past forlorn, burned-out landscapes, industrial ruins, boarded-up buildings, and a huge sign: *Pray—It Works*. About midway through the trip, Jessie began reading the Hitch file. By the time she looked up, the train had arrived in Rhinecliff. Looking out the window of the train at the people on the platform, her eyes came to rest on a tree of a man dressed in a French-cuffed, porcelain-white shirt, snakeskin tie, and Harris Tweed coveralls. This curious combination of London Majesty and high-country Chevron was a dead giveaway, that and his thick, black, perfectly round spectacles. The famous man was an exotic stuffy from the past.

"You must be Mr. Hitch," Jessie said with a knowing smile.

"And you must be Ms. Chandler." The timbre of Valentine's voice sounded patrician. He escorted Jessie to his Pierce-Arrow and opened the door. Jessie got in and sank into the soft leather seat. Valentine gently closed the door and headed back around the car. He settled into the driver's seat and put the touring car into gear.

As they sped south on US Route 9 along the Hudson, Jessie noticed the fragrance of Valentine's cologne. It reminded her of her grandfather's Old Spice, which made her feel comfortable.

"How was your trip?"

"It's the first time I've ever been up here. Next time, I'm buying a oneway ticket."

"I'm a big fan of one-way tickets. Matter of fact, I bought one myself once."

Jessie was surprised by the tawdriness as they crossed the town line into Roosevelt country. The old weathercock atop the Dutch Reformed Church must have witnessed the desecration. One hundred years of luminism had been followed by sixty years of opportunism. Prophets replaced by profits.

Valentine noticed Jessica's dismay. "Sad, isn't it? After the post-war exodus, predators moved in. I recall when the construction crew and bulldozer showed up at the gates of our place. It felt like an invasion of the body snatchers. My mother couldn't understand why anyone in their right mind would cut down the majestic sycamores that had been lining each side of the Post Road since colonial times. As the bulldozer approached the three-hundred-year-old beauties that marked the boundary of our estate, my mother was ready with a porch brick, which she promptly hurled at the oncoming machine. Her brick became the first shot of the revolution."

Jessica looked out the window at what remained of the Franklin Delano Roosevelt Corridor now colonized by the purveyors of Cokes, Daddy Burgers, and outsized onion rings. It looked as if Americana had been buried alive. "I'm looking around, but I'm not seeing much resistance."

"The preservers have been playing defense for too long. Everything you see here, a bulldozer's dream."

"Did you say a bulldozer?"

"The crookery has got to go. All of it. Native Americans had it right from the beginning. The land is owned by the Great Spirit. The problems started when some outsider assumed he owned the place."

Valentine turned left onto a secondary road, which he shared with the abandoned Roosevelt Mall, barely visible through the sheltering old growth. The mall was now a ghost town. Weeds and poison ivy grew in the cracked asphalt. This perpetual problem had existed on the perimeter of the Hitch estate since 1952. While the New Deal had arrived in Crum Elbow in the mid-1930s, in the form of a half million new trees, supervised by Roosevelt himself, unfortunately, his son Elliott saw the future differently. Over a thirteen-month period after his father's death, the county clerk recorded nineteen separate sales of FDR-reforested land earmarked for commercial development.

Valentine turned again, gliding through slightly-tilted, ivy-covered stone gate posts and entering a paradise of rolling hills that reached down to the river. The first structures they came to were ruins: a dilapidated kennel with the windows out. Farther afield, she could just make out the thirty-foot wooden tower for pheasant shoots that had been left to rot after the hunting and shooting had moved further east away from the river after the war. The ladies in their sun hats and parasols were gone too. The stiff formality was long gone, but Jessie could see the potential. "My God, this must have been something in its heyday!"

"It certainly was. Every time I return home, it's upsetting. It's hard to enjoy driving down my own driveway anymore. I'm less concerned about the house. My worry is the legacy of the land."

"Is anyone farming your place? I noticed a grain auger rusting away out there."

"Oh, you know about grain augers?"

"You might be surprised by some of the things I know. I grew up on a farm in Wisconsin. The farm had been in my mother's family since the early 1900s."

"What did you grow?"

"It started out as a dairy farm. My parents are both from the Midwest, but they met at Berkeley in the late sixties. After college, they went back to the farm but not to become farmers. They started a way station for draft dodgers emigrating to Canada. By the end of the war, the farm had become one of the first community-supported agriculture programs. It would be decades before their thinking became part of the mainstream."

Valentine raised his eyebrows. He could feel a slow de-icing. If he were thirty years younger, he might have done something about it. "That certainly is a far cry from the rarified art world."

"I was raised by hippies, then went the other direction. Wound up in Manhattan in the auction business. But, I miss it. Our farm was a Who's Who of herbs, Echinacea, St. John's Wort, American Ginseng, Wormwood, and too many others to mention. We had a full lab in the barn. Those were the days when we would submerge dried herbs like ginseng root in huge vats of the highest proof, do-it-yourself vodka, which was the secret to extracting the medicinal properties. The process took about six months. We had our own brand, Farmer Armor."

"You made tinctures." Valentine loved how the word rolled off his tongue.

"Very good, Mr. Hitch."

"Please, call me Valentine. Were people buying that stuff back then?"

"All medicine was once plant based. That knowledge has always been around. My mother and father were trying to raise consciousness as much as herbs."

"And the family farm?"

"Sold. My father had health problems and priorities changed. Once I moved to the city, I didn't think I'd ever go back to farm the land. But I'm tired of cities."

"It's still a working farm?"

"I'm afraid it's long gone. When we buried my father, I stopped by. It's now a car dealership. The bees and crows are gone. No more apple blossoms. It smells like a gas station."

"That's what I'm trying to prevent from happening here." Valentine took in a breath and exhaled slowly, wondering how much he should tell Jessie. "I'm on the verge of losing this place. It's just unfair. The town board supports corporate developers and religious cults with tax cuts. For what? What are they thinking?" asked the man whose family had fought in the revolution against the British for the first tax break.

Valentine pulled the car around the lawn circle and stopped in front of the stone steps leading up to the house's wide veranda. He walked around to the passenger side of the car, opened the door, and offered Jessie his hand as she stepped out of the Pierce-Arrow.

"Welcome to Burleighwood," Valentine said half-heartedly for what had become a millstone around his neck. He escorted Jessie up the steps.

As Valentine opened the weathered, mahogany door, its brass hinges creaking rather impressively. "I should get these hinges oiled." He had been making that comment for the last two years.

Before Jessie could reach the door, one of her well-shod feet went through a flimsy, rotted floorboard. She caught Valentine's eye.

"That's why you're here. We're in survival mode."

Jessie crossed the threshold. She had been in historic houses before, but there was something different about Burleighwood. The atmosphere of this crumbling old house couldn't have been further away from the slickness of the New York art auction business. Valentine led the way into its deeper reaches. He suddenly stopped and gestured with a dramatic flourish to a painting of his great uncle. "My dear Jessica, lady of New York," he said with a glint in his eye. "Say hello to Humphrey. He was my *Man from U.N.C.L.E*, an uncle's uncle. Humphrey loved every detail about this place. He was like a mighty tree. His roots ran deep."

Jessie looked up at Humphrey staring down from on high. "Hey, don't give me that look."

Valentine chuckled. "Cut Humphrey some slack. Nothing this beautiful has crossed his gaze in ages."

"What did Humphrey do?"

A smile drew across Valentine's lips at the thought of his dapper and flamboyant long-dead great-uncle. "Humphrey lived in the age when the old rule was still in effect."

"What was the old rule?"

"You never asked a gentleman what he did."

"Why not?"

"Because perhaps he didn't *do* anything. Humphrey wasn't suited for any type of work, except for, perhaps, Vaudeville, and no one wanted an actor in the family. Please, after you."

Valentine and Jessie ambled down a stretch of hallway where six portraits of the Revolutionary War heroes by Charles Wilson Peale had once hung on the walls, their silhouettes still visible as darker rectangles on the damask-covered walls. "As you can see, some of your colleagues have already been here."

As much as he hated to do it, Valentine had periodically auctioned off the most valuable paintings in the family collection to keep the tax assessor at bay and sustain Burleighwood. Now that the last Peale had been auctioned, he still had one more painting that was either of no value, or priceless. Either way, Valentine had always treasured it and the idea of parting with it wasn't a great feeling.

They proceeded past the open door of a large, empty ballroom, where a line of Chippendale chairs without cushions, skeletons, were stacked against the wall, a morgue for furniture. Valentine told Jessica of a young FDR whirling around the ballroom with Eleanor in the early twenties.

The painting in question was hanging in the study. The room was painted a shiny Chinese red lacquer and filled with Hitch family treasures from journeys to China: vases and old clocks and tea chests. Shelves along the wall were lined with leather-bound travel logs and books, including the 1877 edition of Noah Webster's dictionary that had been passed down through the family.

Jessie went over to inspect a murky painting of a dancer looking down above an enormous bowed sofa with overstuffed cushions that seemed to preserve the impressions of guests who had sat there a century ago. After a moment, she took it off the wall and carried it over to the window.

"That oil study has always been one of my favorite paintings," Valentine said, tagging close behind her. "I've speculated that it's either worth millions or nothing at all. No one in the family wanted it, which was just fine by me."

"Well, that doesn't surprise me that you have a very good eye," Jessie said, feeling her pulse rise and trying to hide it. She bent closer to examine the painting. She studied the back and took notes. After a few more minutes, she looked up at Valentine. "I don't want to get your hopes up, but there's a chance that this is a very important painting."

"Really? You don't say."

"Don't hold me to this, but it looks like it may be a study by Sargent."

"Well, that wouldn't surprise me. He was a regular fixture around here when my grandmother was alive."

"I'm not making any promises, but if I had to guess, I'd say it just may be the long-lost oil study for his masterpiece, The Spanish Dancer. Sargent scholars agree that the finished version was his most important work. It's hanging in the Isabella Stewart Gardner Museum in Boston. Even the oil study for the painting would be extremely valuable."

"Great Scott! How can we verify this?"

"I'll take some snapshots and show them to Gordon. If he agrees, we'll have our art handlers come up here to crate it so we can ship to New York for authentication."

"How long will that take?"

"It helps that Sargent was in the house, but it's still quite a process. The experts run a battery of tests to confirm date and origins, and then it goes through scholarly peer review."

"If Gordon agrees, will you return with the movers to crate the painting then?"

"Yes, I will, I hope."

"Well then, upon your return, I must give you a tour of the land, farmer to farmer."

"There's nothing I'd love more."

*   *   *

Back in New York, Jessie's photographs of the dancer's strong limbs were hungrily inspected by a gauntlet of experts. No red flags. The following Monday, Jessie took the train up to the Hudson Valley to supervise the art handlers. On the train, just as Jessie was walking to the back of the car, a large hiking boot, leg-attached, blocked her way. Must have been a size fourteen at least. Jessie's gaze led her up the leg to an impressive looking man. Jeff Bridges? Too young to be him, but no doubt a person of consequence. She started to gingerly step over the boot when the giant came alive. He sat up awkwardly dressed in a faded white oxford shirt and khaki pants.

"Looks like a tight squeeze," she said.

"Yeah, it's tough being tall. Japan is the worst."

Jessie smiled and flopped her bag in the seat across the aisle.

The tall man rubbed his eyes and seemed to take in her beauty. He could not stop gazing at her. He kept looking over.

Jessie could feel his eyes and interest. She had already decided that she liked him but felt safer minding her own business.

When the train pulled into Poughkeepsie, Jessie's kindred traveler rose from his seat.

As he passed, she allowed him a deep gaze. "Poughkeepsie?" he inquired.

"Rhinecliff."

He smiled and exited the train.

Valentine arrived with his usual élan in his Pierce-Arrow to pick Jessie up at the train station. The engine sounded louder than Jessie remembered. As they approached town, traffic came to a standstill. Valentine called out over the motor, "The age of leisurely motoring around Crum Elbow is long over. I need a defensive driving course."

When to oil study of the dancer was loaded and ready for its trip back to Manhattan, Valentine asked Jessie, "Do you still have time for a walk?"

"Absolutely," she said.

"Marvelous, let's get out of this dark house. It's such a beautiful day." The meandering dusty farm road branched off to their right past Burleighwood's old farm buildings. They walked by the greenhouse, the stables, and the barn, where spotted cattle had been. Once they reached the overgrown fields, Jessica asked Valentine if Crum Elbow had a farmers market.

"No. Farmers are a dying breed around here."

"That's too bad."

"We've farmed out everything, including our farming. I had always hoped to bring back the farm at Burleighwood."

"I don't see any reason why you couldn't," Jessie said, looking around. She bent over and scooped up a handful of dirt. "This is rich soil. You could grow almost anything here," Jessie said, stopping for a moment to contemplate a weather-worn sign that read "Spotted Cow." She gave Valentine a puzzled look. "You have cows?"

"No, that's a ski hill. I'm afraid the Spotted Cow is overgrown."

"I love to ski. In fact, I'm in the process of moving to Sun Valley. You're my last client."

"Well, I'm glad we met before you moved out West."

"I feel the same way, Valentine."

Valentine concluded his tour of the grounds by proposing to take Jessie on the network of paths that connected the various parts of the estate. "Let's take the fairy path home, and I'll show you the strawberry fields."

"Fairies and Strawberry Fields."

"Oh, this place is rife with life. All kinds of entities have lived here for centuries, including me. The strawberries are this way," Valentine said, pointing ahead. They followed the curving path through the woods to a higher elevation, where the small, luscious berries had been warmed like a June afternoon. "I love the little ones nestled in the upper stems of the plant closer to the sun. They're so tiny," Valentine said.

"The smaller the better for the fairies."

After the tasting, they decided to leave some berries for the fairies and continued down a path heavily carpeted with pine needles, which eventually led through the walled garden to the house.

As they approached the west porch, a figure stood up. Jeff Bridges from the train. Again?

"Livy! What a fabulous surprise. Jessie, please meet my elusive nephew."

"We're old friends," Jessie said, raising her eyebrows.

Livy bear hugged Valentine and then wrapped his arms around Jessie as well. "I'm fresh in from LA. We're more effusive out there."

"Elusive and effusive. I like that," Jessie said.

"That would be me. Livy Hitch at your service."

"Your nephew got off in Poughkeepsie. Wouldn't have believed that I'd see him again, let alone an hour later," Jessica said, then looked at him intently.

"It's usually easier to get a cab from Poughkeepsie," Livy said.

Once everyone was comfortably settled on the porch, Valentine disappeared into the house. Livy wondered if Jessie was Valentine's girlfriend. "How do you know Valentine?"

"I'm with Sotheby's."

"Please don't tell me he's selling Burleighwood."

"No, I'm here on other business."

"Thankfully, I'm not ready for that conversation."

"When was the last time you visited your uncle?"

"It's probably been about six months. I usually see Valentine two or three times a year."

"Were you raised here?"

"I wasn't that lucky. We just came to Crum Elbow for the month of August, Christmas, and a couple of times during the year."

"So how do you feel about the old place?"

"It's a strange brew. When my grandmother was alive, it was like Buckingham Palace. Every time I came into the room, I was required to bow my head before speaking. I hated it. It was awful. But out in Los Angeles I kind of miss the old rules."

"Too *LA*issez-faire?"

"Ha, yes, something like that. Maybe it takes living in LA to realize that decorum is what holds the universe together. My trips to Burleighwood kept my life in balance. Throughout the eighties and nineties, I'd fly into New York for voiceover recordings and then set out on the Rip Van Winkle Express train up the Hudson."

Jessie shrugged her shoulders. "Never take Burleighwood for granted. When I moved to New York, the family farm was sold out from under me."

That sent a shiver down Livy's spine. California may have been a great place for reinventing, but he always came back to Burleighwood to ground himself. Long runs on the carriage trails would remind Livy of the restorative power of being home. The estate's carriage roads, and undulating trails down to the river, had different personalities. There was the apple blossom orchard path, the run to the ice pond, the sinking earth of Mosley's marsh, the sheltering canopy of the Norway Spruce, and the hop over the railroad tracks for a quick dip in the cool waters of Crum Elbow Creek. "How many generations of your family farmed the land?"

"Three. My mother inherited the family dairy farm from her parents that had come originally from my great-grandmother."

Valentine returned with a tray of champagne glasses and a bottle of sparkling wine from a local vineyard, but Livy only wanted to gaze at Jessie.

Valentine filled the three glasses, then set the bottle down on the outdoor wicker coffee table. "Did you tell Livy about the oil sketch?"

"In my business, loose lips sink ships. I did mention I worked for Sotheby's."

"Well, I'm trying not to get overly excited, but there's a chance we found an important painting in the study. Jessie has come up here to arrange for its trip to New York. You remember it. The naked dancer that was over the sofa in the study."

"My first legal peak at the female body. Obviously, you hadn't found the painting when you wrote me last, Valentine?" Livy looked at Jessie. Jessie looked back at Livy. The wine continued to flow.

Suddenly, Jessie excused herself to make a phone call to her office. When she was out of earshot, Livy looked over at Valentine. "Jessica's got it going on. Is she married?"

"You'd think so, but there's no ring. When I met her, I thought she might be right for you."

"Well, here I am."

"Let's have dinner and then you can accompany Jessie back on the train and get to know her. Although it's probably good for you to know she's moving to Sun Valley."

"Well, Idaho isn't so far away. Thank you, Uncle. The only person that's been looking after me lately is my agent."

"What? No woman in your life?"

"Plenty, I guess. Maybe I'm not ready to settle down."

"That's probably because you haven't met the right one. Well, don't break this one's heart. She's special."

When Jessie returned, Valentine moved the party to the overlook on the bluff where he had watched the sunset over the Hudson all of his life. The path to the lookout had been well trod for centuries. Valentine's happiest memories were of breaking bread on the bluff with those he loved best. Infinity, somehow, felt more accessible to him as the setting sun passed through the ice of his cocktail into the warmth of his heart.

Valentine lifted his glass. "To the secret the dancer keeps."

Livy nodded. "To the naked lady."

Jessie chimed in. "To Burleighwood."

No more needed to be said. They sat in the spell of the sun setting over the slow-moving river. Valentine looked up and the sky seemed unusually populated with large birds: ravens, hawks, an all-American Bald Eagle. He finally broke the silence. "Mosley has orchestrated an impromptu dinner. Shall we adjourn to the dining room?"

As the purple darkness set in, they moved once again back to the house and gathered around the large, mahogany dining room table that seated twenty-two. That number had not sat at this table since Margaret Hitch's last dinner party in 1976. The faded green walls with gold leaf trim had not been updated since the last century. The wooden floors were partially covered by a worn, nearly threadbare oriental rug that extended the length of the room.

"Please," Valentine said to Jessie, gesturing to the chair to the right of the head while Livy sat to Valentine's left across from Jessie. "Livy, if you would please serve the red wine, I'll check on dinner," Valentine said and disappeared into the kitchen. He returned, and soon thereafter, a tall, slender, elegant man entered the room from the kitchen.

"Livy, welcome back. My name is Mosley," he said, introducing himself to Jessie. "Dinner is about to be served. I hope everyone likes venison. It was killed by bow on this property," he said before returning to the kitchen.

Valentine turned to Jessie, "If you spend any time here, you'll find Burleighwood to be a bit otherworldly. And Mosley certainly helps keep it that way."

"Does he live here, Valentine?"

"Oh, yes. He was born here. I've known Mosley my entire life. He's a charming man. Mosley revels in the lag somewhere around the end of the Second World War and the 1960s."

Valentine excused himself and returned to the kitchen to help Mosley serve dinner. They set down plates of venison chops, wild rice, and a cool cucumber salad. "I hope this meets with everyone's satisfaction," Mosley said and sat down at the table.

"Brilliant Mosley, are you the hunter?" Livy asked.

"No, this is the work of our former Special Forces mechanic, Tad," Mosley said, sitting down next to Jessie.

Taking a bite, Livy smiled, surprised. "Tender."

"Yes, and not a bit gamey," Mosley said, dipping his fingers into a glass bowl of warm water and drying them on his frayed damask napkin.

Livy reached for the bottle. The local white wines were great, but when it came to red wine, Valentine was partial to Bordeaux. "Red, Jessie?"

"Why not? Valentine said I might recognize your voice, Livy, and I do." Jessie raised her eyebrows. "Good to the last drop."

"Ah, you have a good ear."

"And you have a memorable voice."

"Maxwell House pays the bills. Freelancing can be a beast. But I'm too ADHD to work in an office."

"No one in my family thought I'd end up working in an office."

"What were they expecting?"

"Well, they didn't expect me to move to New York."

"Where did they think you'd end up?"

"Closer to the earth. But coming out of college, the idea of living on a farm didn't appeal to me. I had too much to prove to myself. I needed to find my own way."

"Valentine told me you're moving to Sun Valley. That's a big move."

"It's time."

After dessert and coffee, Mosley opened the kitchen door, then paused to check his watch. "Just a reminder, Livy and Jessie, if you are planning to make the 7:50 to New York, you'll have to leave in twenty minutes."

Livy excused himself to use the washroom. He proceeded down a long hallway nearly as wide as the entrance hall past the closed-off ballroom where newsprint was taped to the inside of the red French doors. The former glory of that house made it too big to heat.

Like Mosley, Valentine, in many ways, had also purposely not changed with the times, particularly. In the Pierce-Arrow on the way to the train station, Livy looked over at Valentine. "I'm surprised you haven't bought a new car in the last fifty years."

"Oh, there will never be another Pierce-Arrow."

"Yes, but the newer cars are much safer and use less gas."

"I'd never sell it," Valentine said.

"The leather seats, the walnut interior, such a work of art," Jessie said in disagreement with Livy.

"In LA you'd get run over," Livy added.

Valentine dropped Jessie and Livy at the train station, where they caught the Amtrak out of Poughkeepsie to Pennsylvania Station.

They had to walk through two cars to find seats together. Once they had settled in beside each other, Jessie asked Livy who he was in town auditioning for.

"The real thing, Coca-Cola."

"That's a big account."

"They were my original account. I actually worked on the launch of New Coke."

"What ever happened to New Coke?"

"The brand failed. It wanted to out-hip Pepsi, but the fad didn't last. All the Coke loyalists insisted on going back to the classic formula and Norman Rockwell."

"I've never met a veteran of the cola wars."

"It was never really a war. It was more like a drive-by shooting. The only casualty was New Coke."

"I guess the real thing turned out to be bottled water."

"That came later. We were before the Internet; we had a captive audience. Everyone watched the same commercials, drank the same soda, and knew the lyrics to the same songs. All the brand choices were binary. We had Colgate and Crest in the toothpaste category."

"I used Pepsodent and drank Mountain Dew."

"Well, Mountain Dew is Pepsi in disguise, and Pepsodent? Well, with your smile, whatever you're using is working."

Jessie smiled back into the secret depths of his eyes. He could feel her looking into his heart. His heaviness lifted.

"Are you happy in California?"

Livy realized at that moment that he had never asked himself that question. She was looking into the self-reflecting pool that he avoided. Out the window to their right, the Hudson flowed on.

Livy and Jessie popped into a yellow cab, and he dropped her off in front of her building. Jessie lived in a brownstone apartment on a treelined block off Fifth Avenue. Livy promised to stay in touch. He leaned forward to kiss her on the cheek. She turned slightly, and their lips met. She whispered, "I have a feeling we're going to see each other again."

CHAPTER 4

The era of hierarchy and the class system did not end with World War II. It was replaced by a curious meritocracy that spawned our current day crooks.

—Valentine Hitch, *Crook's Paradise*

Two years later Valentine's painting was declared a rare find and sold at auction.

Two years later, the oil study of the Spanish Dancer was authenticated as a work by John Singer Sargent. It was declared a rare find and sold at auction. When the gavel came down, it sold for four million dollars, the highest price ever paid for a Sargent oil study. When Valentine heard the news, he breathed a long sigh and made himself a double Manhattan. After all, Manhattan had been very kind to him. With cocktail in hand, Valentine sat his royal bottom down at his black Underwood typewriter but then decided he'd better write it by hand. He paused for a moment, wondering what the day was. He seldom needed to know the date. He dug out a World Wildlife Fund calendar buried in the stack of mail on his desk, smiled, and began writing.

Feb. 20, 2003

Dear Scavengers,

Sorry, but you're not going to get your grubby hands on Burleighwood. My grounds are not going to be turned over to the state. I have the honor to inform you that I am paying in full my back taxes, including all penalties and interest. Should there be a problem, you know where to contact me. God knows you have before.

No longer truant,

Valentine Hitch, Photographer at Large

Over the next two years, Burleighwood entered the twenty-first century with an electrical upgrade, new plumbing, and rooftop solar and geothermal heating and cooling. Valentine had also donated a stretch of land along the river to the Green Borders Conservancy. They were attempting to link all the undeveloped land along the Hudson from Yonkers to Troy to form what they called the Emerald Necklace. Valentine also had compassion for his master mechanic, Tad Robbins, when he came home from our War on Terror with his leg blown off. His former job wasn't available. When Valentine heard that Tad had been injured, he tracked him down and brought him to Burleighwood and offered him one of the barns to set up shop.

Valentine had been slowly plotting the future of Burleighwood beyond his lease he called life. Now his biggest concerns were finding out what might be lurking next door at Crumwold Hall, Colonel Archibald Rogers's former estate, and gathering some evidence for his swan song, *Crook's Paradise*. Valentine had always believed that the soul of Crum Elbow was not dead, just hiding out in places like Crumwold Hall. Of course, the "Crum" is derived from Crum Elbow. As a boy, Franklin D. Roosevelt had been tutored and often played in Crumhold's tower room. The family had left in the late 1930s, after Colonel Rogers's life came to a sudden end when his dog leapt out of his open-air car to chase after a squirrel. It was the last time the estate had been run by a family of means. In the early forties, the mansion housed President Roosevelt's security detail to protect him from U-boats and assassins. Crumhold's Great Hall had served as a secret meeting place for Churchill and Roosevelt during the war, as stuffed mountain goats, wildcats, and moose heads peered

down with Adirondack authority. In the fifties, suburbia had rolled itself out like AstroTurf, over family, farm, and polo fields, unchallenged. By the early eighties, a twelve-foot-high chain-link fence topped with rolled razor wire had been installed, separating Crumwold from its neighbors. So much for fireside chatting. Valentine wasn't sure if this fence was to keep people out, or in. The so-called religious group currently occupying the Rogers family hearth had battened down like a doomsday cult. They were not interested in Bible preaching or free turkeys. Valentine certainly believed in the separation of church and state, but in this case, he saw too much separation.

One night, a curious sound coming from the neighboring Crumwold woods awakened Valentine. He opened the window and could hear distant voices above the din of diesel engines and periodic grinding of gears, as if dump trucks were making the steep climb up from the river. He wondered whether God had been taken out of the equation next door. Normally, Valentine would have grabbed his camera, found a flashlight, and been halfway through the woods to complete final due diligence for his life work. Alas, he had come to the solemn conclusion that his days of tracking photographs at any cost were over. Most of the photographers of his generation were long gone. Sure, he could walk next door and snap the shutter. The problems would start if he had to make a fast getaway. Still, recent developments could not be ignored. He was no stranger to this feeling. It had nearly cost him his life several times. He closed the window and reluctantly went back to bed.

By early the next evening, Valentine had convinced himself that it would be safe enough to spy from the Crumwold woods. He found a lookout spot near the edge of the tree line for optimum surveillance. He had no idea what the heck was going on with all those lights coming from the old camp on the river where the Colonel had long ago launched his iceboat, *Jack Frost*. What compelled Valentine's inner Sherlock the most was the tower light. He noted that the tower light was the only light in the dark abandoned chateau. He suspected the tower was the brains of the operation, and he would need a photograph of whomever the crook was in the tower. It was certainly going to be more dangerous than any photo taken from the safety of the tree line. He needed another version of himself, only a generation younger, who could handle risky business, run, and never look back. As a matter of fact, the photographer that came to mind for the job owed him a favor.

There was only one problem: Hollis Dixon was in rehab.

The next day, Valentine set a course for the Synergy Center, north on US Route 9, which ran alongside the Hudson. He needed to make a quick stop at the New Deal Diner to pick up a gift. All the parking spots were full, so he continued up the street and parked in front of the James Roosevelt Free Library. As Valentine got out of the car, the skunk smell of marijuana overpowered his nose like a cow patty on his shoe. The misfit skateboarders had become local mystics. Their chillums and their jeans were all they needed. One boy stood out. Tanner had long blond hair tucked up under his Rasta-colored hat. Valentine had enjoyed watching Tanner's progress on the skateboard over the summer. Tanner spent his days and nights grinding the handrails and other features in their suburban landscape. Valentine thought the flagpole in front of the town hall might be next.

Turns out Tanner had yet to ride the virgin and sacrosanct handrails of FDR's wheelchair ramp to the library. Valentine was stopped by one of the resident wags with pants half-on (or maybe it was pants half-off) as his compatriot launched with a kick flip onto the handrail. Stacked over his ballsy feet, pupils flared, his hipness shot past Valentine, and glided all the way down the handrail and stuck the landing.

"Boys, I'm concerned about your future," Valentine said, smiling wryly. He had no clue how much money could be made in their airborne teenage universe. Tanner had a tremendous work ethic to match his creative mind. He'd told Valentine that he dreamed of qualifying for the X Games and the sponsorship of Red Bull or Oakley.

Zachary, the philosopher of the rail yard, looked at Valentine. "We *are* the future, Valentine."

The New Deal Diner, a little tin-roofed establishment on the corner of Fulton and Route 9, had been there since the fifties. It was the first eyesore to pop up after the war, but it was tame compared to the emergence of neon-roof chickens and golden arches. Cosmo Papas, the second-generation owner, had survived the invasion of drive-by eating. He was willing to bet that there were still those who preferred busty waitresses to Styrofoam. Cosmo approached the counter with the big smile of a man dressed in a "hang loose" happy shirt. "Hey, Valentine. What will it be? Coffee? Lunch? The rib roast just came out of the oven."

"I wish I could join you, Cosmo, but what I really need is a six-pack of Coca-Cola. Also, please add four lottery tickets."

"Smart move, Valentine. It's up to sixty-five million."

Valentine turned his attention to a table in the far corner. Homer Grubb Junior had planted himself and was holding court behind the shelter of a broken jukebox. As Valentine awaited his order, he watched person after person arrive, go to Junior Grubb's corner, and deliver all kinds of bags. At one point, Grubb opened one of the duffels and counted a wad of bills. Valentine was no longer shocked by such public behavior. During his lifetime, he had watched the town that his family had practically started go from having a rigid class system to being rigidly crass, and some really shaky middle ground had erupted, too.

Valentine left with the lottery tickets and handed one to each of the skateboarders. "Gentlemen, since we're all gamblers, I thought we'd make it official. Lottery tickets for each of you."

Usually, Valentine provided them something to drink, usually peach Snapple. The boys loved Valentine, and he loved them. The man who had the most to be snooty about was the only person in Crum Elbow who would acknowledge them.

Valentine got back in his Pierce-Arrow and followed the signs for the Synergy Center. The New Age euphemism for rehab made him chuckle. Valentine knew that his one true disciple, Hollis Dixon, had for some time been stymied and depressed over his life and photography. It took life-threatening situations for Hollis to forget his pain and respond fully in the moment. Hollis had been most alive when he was getting his skull cracked open while covering race riots and the Vietnam War. He had photographed the marches and police brutality in the South. He had been present for the Chicago riots and the Kent State massacre. He had had his camera broken and had been tear-gassed, clubbed, and thrown in jail. On countless occasions, Valentine had posted bail for Hollis and provided him with new cameras. News services and major magazines picked up Hollis's images. They were seen across the country and throughout the world. Valentine couldn't have been prouder.

By the late 1970s, Hollis had become a featured photojournalist for *Rolling Stone* at the height of its popularity and influence. During the 1980s, he traveled the world photographing rock stars. He was internationally recognized and began living a life that he would never have dreamed of growing up a poor Black kid in rural Mississippi. Hunter S. Thompson was a close friend and consistent bad influence. Hollis became a fixture at Hunter's Woody Creek compound in Aspen. Hunter taught Hollis to fire a gun and blow things up while tripping on mescaline. In the late eighties, Hollis went to work for *Vanity Fair*. He then lived on champagne and cocaine. By that time, he and Valentine had lost touch.

The Synergy Center was located on the Hudson river in the once decrepit Rhinecliff Hotel, built in 1854. In recent years, intrepid New Agers had radically transformed the three-story, wooden structure into what they called "a sanctuary for healing." Valentine admired how this funky old hotel had been repurposed. He steered the car as if he were framing a photograph of the historic building. Valentine strode through the old hotel entrance and noted a change in the faded decor. He also found himself falling in love with the green-eyed yogini at the welcome desk. She handed him a visitor's pass and directed him to the day spa in the new wing.

Valentine held up the six-pack of Coke and flashed her a mischievous smile. "Is this allowed?"

"I'm looking the other way." She winked.

Valentine thanked his new friend and found Hollis coming out of the changing room. Hollis was wearing a paisley bow tie. One would never suspect that he was once an antiestablishment activist. The bow tie was Hollis's homage to his mentor, Valentine Hitch. It reflected Valentine's simple, gentlemanly code of honor that Hollis had been saved by and absorbed. Hollis appeared to be startled when he saw his old friend. "Valentine, what are you doing here?"

Valentine could detect the lingering fluorocarbons of whatever Hollis had recently sprayed on himself. "I tracked you down, brother. I have a favor to ask. I can't believe you've been here all this time and you didn't call."

"Well, as I remember, the last time I was in rehab, you were so pissed off that I went back to drinking, you told me not to call you anymore. You said you were done with me."

"Well, I must have been drinking. You know I love you, Hollis."

Whatever healing Hollis had done was still in process. "I think I've gotten to the core of my blackness."

"Your depression?"

"No, my skin color," Hollis grimaced. The world Hollis grew up in had been a hostile place: "Separate but equal" had been the doctrine of the land. From water fountains to schools, the American South had been totally segregated.

Hollis shrugged his shoulders. "They have a different approach than the medical model. This is more spiritual."

"That's great, but how about the drinking?"

"My desire has been neutralized."

"That's a new one for me."

"There's a lot of pain to resolve in my lineage. You may have lost me for a while, but I hope I haven't lost what you saw in me."

"Talent is talent. You may block it for a while, but it's going to bust through at some point."

"You know, a couple of months ago, just before I checked in here, it all hit me. I went to an exhibition at my old artists' co-op downtown in Greenwich Village, the one you helped fund when I got out of art school."

Valentine smiled. "I remember. The good old days: you and a couple dozen other starving optimists."

"That was right before the shit hit the fan, and LBJ sent another quarter-million high school kids into Vietnam," Hollis added.

"If I recall correctly, it was the same year they took *Mister Ed* off the air. No more talking horses to entertain America over TV dinners. No more Ed, just war dead. So, you visited the old studio," Valentine said.

"I met a provocative young photographer. His work had freshness and originality. He was way out of the mainstream. For better or worse, he knew my work and asked me to autograph the latest volume of my photos. I opened the book and began leafing through page after page of portraits of international celebrities, one big face after another, beautifully art-directed but soulless. It turned my stomach to see how far I'd drifted. You don't understand. The camera is no longer my friend."

"Yes, but *I* am. You need a home. Why don't you come live at Burleighwood?"

"Seriously?"

"Come stay for a while."

Hollis couldn't really think of any place he'd rather be. He felt like Noah himself had invited him onto his mighty ark.

Two weeks later, Hollis checked his sober-self out and hopped in Valentine's ride. Valentine was happy to have his old friend back but had set certain ground rules: no guns, no gonzo, and nothing stronger than ganja.

As Valentine turned right through the gateposts and proceeded down the tree-bordered drive, Hollis was delighted. "Just being here makes me feel better."

"This isn't exactly the Wild West."

"I know you're not a fan of Hunter."

"Not when it comes to you. I can't deny that he was a great writer, particularly in the earlier years. Tom Wolfe saw even more Mark Twain in Hunter than himself, even though he was the one wearing the white suit."

"I was gonzo before I met Gonzo," Hollis said, looking out the window. He was surprised that the undergrowth had been culled and cut back, and in the distance, he could see that the fields had been planted. "Valentine, I didn't know you had a magic wand."

"You've been away from Burleighwood for a long time, stranger. There are some big changes afoot."

"What's Mosley looking at?" Hollis asked, looking toward the field.

Valentine looked out the car window and saw the now familiar scene of Mosley with his binoculars raised, a field guide bulging out of his vest pocket. "He's looking up into the leaves, trying to find a window into the warblers. He answers now to the call of the wild. Like Burleighwood, he, himself, has become a bird sanctuary. These days you don't find him around the house much except at meal times. Mosley no longer eats in the kitchen; that era of hierarchy is over. After my mother died, I ended the class system at Burleighwood. I released the staff, but Mosley chose to stay."

"And serve?"

"We all serve, Hollis."

"Dinner?"

"Dinner, yes. And when my mother died, he also stayed on to serve the beauty."

"Like fresh flowers and finger bowls."

"The whole nine yards. Mosley was born into it as much as I was. He knew intuitively that there was no better place to be. We relaxed the rules and divvied up the duties. Mosley preferred cooking and serving. I took charge of the vacuum cleaner and tried to fix things, though I was never known for my home mechanics."

"Does he ever leave the property?"

"Mosley is up at dawn birding, but he doesn't have to go far to find just about every species in Dutchess County. The farthest he travels is north to find the sneaky Clapper and Virginia Rails in the marshes near Thompson's Pond."

"FDR had always been interested in birds."

"Yes, as a boy he roamed the same places spotting birds."

Hollis let his gaze take in the surroundings. "This place has a new feeling."

"It does indeed, in the form of a beautiful, organic farmer. You can't miss her. She's got auburn hair and drives a beat-up, light-blue Ford pickup."

"Now you've really sparked my interest. How long has she been here?"

"Not long. It's an interesting story. She discovered the painting."

"A farmer discovered John Singer Sargent?"

"Well, she wasn't a farmer at the time. She was an American paintings expert in New York. She was sent up here by Sotheby's. Her name is Jessica Chandler. It was serendipity. It turns out this was her last assignment. She was in the process of leaving the auction business and moving to Sun Valley."

"Then how did she end up here?"

"She came up here and fell in love with the land. She was just as happy to discover the farm as the Sargent painting. I think her visit to Burleighwood confirmed that she was done with New York. When she moved out West, she stayed in touch. It was as if she hadn't left. She called regularly. Her missives from the mountaintop assured me that she was fully back in her element. I was amazed that hot dogging had become an Olympic sport."

"And?"

"There was a stretch where she went radio silent. I expected she had met someone. When she got back in touch, she told me she was done with resort skiing. Peace and beauty were her aim. Slowly but surely, she found her new home, but it wasn't in 'Fun Valley'. One day there was a knock on the door. I almost didn't recognize this wholesome face and ruddy enthusiasm. I looked down and took a mental snapshot of Jessie's brown suede Chelsea boots in the loam of Burleighwood. In a flash, I saw her in overalls and muddy red wellies working the land."

"It's hard enough to move from the farm to Manhattan, but it's even more bizarre going from table back to farm."

"Jessie's just so unique. You're really going to enjoy her."

"I can't wait to meet her."

"This is her first season. She's only been at it a few months."

"Does she have good help?"

"Oh, yeah. Jessie has already attracted an eclectic assortment of workers, various kinds of refugees from city life. She has an entrepreneurial male friend who comes up to help with the weeding once a week, ostensibly to get his hands in the earth, but I think he has other intentions."

"No matter how much art you create or find, your collection of people has always been an art in itself," Hollis mused, mostly to himself. "Speaking of, how's Livingston?"

After a moment, Valentine said, "He used to visit Burleighwood a couple of times a year. He hasn't been back to New York in two years. The voice-over profession has tanked. Famous actors and actresses are stealing his work."

"He'll be back. The prodigal son always returns."

"In the meantime, you'll have to meet our resident mechanic, Tad Robbins. I offered him his own room, but he prefers to sleep in the hayloft beneath the ridge of the barn roof. He claims the commute from the main house is too long. He's fearless. After 9/11, Tad enlisted in the army. He *wanted* to fight for our country."

After a few switchbacks, the full panorama of the river came into view. Valentine pulled up along the side of an enormous, freshly painted green barn with white clover-leaf molding and gave the horn a couple of toots. When Jessica moved to Burleighwood, she and Valentine had worked together side by side for months to make the space livable. During this time, their bond had deepened. Jessica stepped through the French doors and came down the steps to greet her visitors. "Well, hello, Jessie. I want to introduce you to my old friend Hollis Dixon."

Jessica extended her hand. "You mean *the* Hollis?"

"That's me. I'd forgotten just how beautiful the view of the Hudson is down here."

"People are discovering the Hudson Valley again," Jessica said, speaking as part of the new wave. "Well, it's great to meet you, Hollis," Jessie said, then told Hollis and Valentine that she had some plants to water and off she went.

Valentine eased the Pierce-Arrow around the lawn circle and came to a full stop at the front steps to drop Hollis off. "I'm going to put the car back in the barn. I'll meet you in a few minutes."

Hollis climbed the front steps with noticeably less alacrity than he had once had. He paused at the front door and noted the irony of the moment. Here he was once again at Valentine's front door. Hollis summed up his journey thus far in three words: "rags, riches, rehab."

CHAPTER 5

The biggest threat to our survival is us, and our incompatibility
with the natural order.

—Valentine Hitch, *Crook's Paradise.*

Now all these years later, Hollis awakened feeling the snakelike
movement of grace moving through his body. He rolled over. He could
also feel the years of abuse embedded in his sixty-one-year-old body.

When Hollis appeared at the kitchen door, Valentine looked up from
his writing. "Welcome home, Hollis."

"Sure, feels good," Hollis responded.

Valentine smiled. "Please join me."

Just then, Mosley appeared at the pantry door. "Hollis, my dear man. Welcome back."

"You're very kind, Mosley. It's great to see you."

"Feelings are mutual."

"This is the one place I really feel at home."

"Time moves slow like the river here," Mosley said. "How about a cup of coffee?"

Hollis sat down across from Valentine. "That would be great. For the last two weeks I've been drinking wheatgrass juice."

"You're detoxing gonzo out of your liver." Valentine said, then laughed. Remember those springs I've been trying to get you to go to for decades, you stubborn old goat? They'll restore you, Hollis. I'm taking you to meet the Earth Mother."

"When did you start spouting New Age doo-dah?"

"This is ancient doo-dah," Valentine chuckled.

Hollis sighed. "Maybe those springs will fill up my cup. It just never feels full."

Valentine finished his coffee and turned to Hollis. "Ready for our walkabout?"

"I could use the fresh air."

"Mosley, thank you for breakfast. We'll see you at dinner. Happy birding."

Valentine was probably the only person in Crum Elbow who did not drink the town water. He was certainly the only one who drove north to Eleanor Roosevelt's grandparents' old property and then hiked with empty half-gallon jugs out to the long-forgotten Livingston springs. Since the well that had sustained Burleighwood for over a century had dried up, Valentine had been making the hike to the springs once weekly. The water that came out of the tap was fine for everyday usage. But, for drinking, Valentine preferred God's sweetest water. It came out of the earth diamond pure.

As they drove north toward the town of Tivoli, Hollis tried to read Valentine's mind, to no avail. "Valentine, what's up with that favor you wanted? Don't tell me you want me to be your water boy."

"No, not yet anyway. I have a more important job for you."

"What's the job?"

"The crooks have moved in next door."

"You want me to capture a crook?"

"No, I need you to shoot one …"

Hollis's expression was of a long corridor of pain.

"With a camera. I've come to the realization that I'm not James Bond anymore, Hollis."

"I came to that realization a long time ago."

"Dammit, Hollis, I need you to click the shutter for me."

"I can't even look at a camera."

"Forget the camera. Just look into the viewfinder. I've been up nights worrying about my book. I fear my message won't survive. I've been working on it, Hollis, for forty years, since the day Aldous Huxley died, November 22, 1963; a president died that day, too. In fact, the whole country died that day."

"Sorry Valentine, I can't … just can't."

Crossing over Crum Elbow Creek, Valentine powered north into history itself. About ten miles up the River Road, they passed Steen Valeje, the estate once owned by the Republican side of the Roosevelt family known to periodically boo FDR. Then, just up the road were the entrance gates to Rokeby, an early Camelot funded by John Jacob Astor's fortune. Farther up the Hudson, Valentine passed a series of gatehouses that marked the entrances of the former country places of his Livingston ancestors. He finally turned up a steep hill and proceeded past a yellow brick gatehouse and down a gravel driveway passing post-war discordance. The only passable trail to the Livingston springs began on the country place known to history as Oak Terrace. The estate had originally been the home of Eleanor Roosevelt's maternal grandparents, the Halls. Eleanor came to live there when she was five years old, after her mother died of diphtheria. The house had been playing hide and seek with its relevance to the Roosevelt family for the second-half of the twentieth century.

Valentine parked the Pierce-Arrow, and they each grabbed a water jug and walked down the carriage road to the old mansard-roofed, second empire mansion surrounded by scaffolding.

The only passable path to the springs was located behind the historic house. Valentine led Hollis around the perimeter of the house and through an opening in the high garden wall. Skunk cabbage was in full bloom along the trail. They could see and smell clover. Black-capped chickadees called plaintively in the trees. Hitch's footsteps lightened, as he gestured toward a woodchuck, "Ah, life along the Hudson."

The two men paused on the trail where the view of the river opened up with the blue haze of the Catskill Mountains in the distance. Valentine marveled. "Should have brought our cameras."

Hollis grunted with a smile.

Valentine led the way through the dense underbrush to pick up the trail down the hill toward the springs. It wasn't long before Valentine had to sit down for a moment. "The spring just isn't in my legs like it used to be."

"Well, there's always Costco."

"Never."

Valentine rose to his feet and slowly picked his path through the underbrush and low-hanging branches. They descended to a smaller rock ledge, and suddenly, Valentine gestured down where the sparkling water bubbled up. Ignoring the *No Trespassing* sign, Valentine scooped up a handful of cold, clear water and encouraged Hollis to do the same.

Hollis created a cup with his hands and took a sip. He looked out over the water to see a long, black watersnake sunning itself on a rock. Hollis was startled, and so was the snake. They both took off, leaving fearless Valentine standing at the edge of the spring, amused by it all.

Suddenly, a youthful face appeared on an antenna of a body, with buttoned-up authority in his dark green park service uniform. The only merit badge on his uniform was a pine tree patch logo. Valentine recognized the man immediately. "Beano!"

"Great to see you, Vallie."

Hollis returned, shaking his head. "Hollis, meet my old friend, Beano."

"Nice to meet you, Hollis. My name is Benedicto Alessandro, but Valentine has always called me Beano, short for string-Beano."

"We go back a long way," Valentine explained. "When he first came back from the Army, his family was eager to reclaim him."

"Like many Italian families, it's hard to escape the family business, but I finally did it."

"Beano helped us move the gate posts and plant trees to block the mall. When we finally finished, all we could see was a single street light from the edge of the parking lot."

"Not for long. Your mother went to the town board and had it removed within a week."

"I wish everything were as easy as removing a streetlight. So, Beano, you finally discovered the springs."

"I'm security now."

"Not property manager?"

"That was during the renovation. Now I'm security. A patrol car of one."

"*Wow*. What's that like?" asked Valentine.

"More rules, more regs. Vallie, I hate to break it to you, but the springs are off limits."

"What? Why? There hasn't been a problem up until now."

"It's a liability issue."

"Man has drawn water from these springs since Neolithic times. The Native Americans considered it holy water."

"Well, the lawyers consider it a liability. Look, Val, I'm only doing my job. Jillian Flintlock saw you trespassing. She's the head of the Friends of Eleanor Roosevelt (FOEs), a group of do-gooders committed to furthering their heroine's humanitarian efforts."

Valentine turned to Hollis. "Well then, let's go and have a chat with Ms. Flintlock."

The two men picked their way through the brush and brambled back up the hill toward the main house. Beano followed along. They climbed to the second floor, knocked, and stepped into Flintlock's office.

A slight, well-dressed man crossed the room to meet Valentine. "I'm Emerson Winks, the director here, and this is my colleague, Jillian Flintlock. How can we help you?"

"I'm Valentine Hitch, and this is my friend, Hollis Dixon. Seems we have a little misunderstanding here."

"And what might that be?"

"Officer Alessandro has informed me that I can no longer draw water from the spring."

"We now own the property, and you're going to have to get your water like everyone else does: from the faucet," Ms. Flintlock said dismissively.

"As much as I would like to accommodate you, Mr. Hitch, as a public entity, we can't be responsible if you drink the water and get sick, or worse," Winks added.

"Look, we're all *friends of Eleanor*. My family and the Roosevelts were neighbors. My grandmother was one of Eleanor's best friends. Eleanor gave her childhood bed to my grandmother when the Hall family left Oak Terrace, for Pete's sake."

Flintlock's whole face brightened. "We've been looking for that bed!" She rummaged through her desk drawers, pulled out a manila folder, and held up a photograph. "Is this the bed?"

"That's the one," Valentine said, bemused. "It's not as if I've been holding it hostage."

"Did you hear what he said? The bed is practically in our own backyard!"

"Haven't seen the bed in years. Probably buried in one of our back barns," Valentine noted.

"We absolutely *must* have that bed," Ms. Flintlock demanded.

"I'm your only hope."

"How about this? You sign a waiver absolving us of any liability. Water rights for the bed," Winks winked.

Valentine stood up a little taller. "Mr. Winks, we have a deal."

But on the trip back from the springs, Valentine sulked. Without Hollis's help, his biggest fear was that his unfinished manuscript would wind up lost and forgotten in one of Burleighwood's historic barns for seventy-five years, like Eleanor's bed. His only alternative to recruiting Hollis was taking that damn picture himself. Crossing Crum Elbow Creek, he and Hollis approached a red car with the word "CACKLE" emblazoned on its license plates. It was parked on the side of Route 9 south, where the clear view of the river meets the road.

"I was hoping to see that car. Must be my lucky day." Valentine said, and then parked the Pierce-Arrow behind the giant red *Cackle Burger* of a car.

"I'll be right back," Valentine assured Hollis.

And indeed, it was Obie Obermeyer rolling down the window of his 1960 Coupe DeVille Cadillac. Valentine had guessed right. "Hello I'm Valentine Hitch. I'm guessing you're Mr. Obermeyer?" he said with a wry smile.

"You got me." He looked at Valentine buttoned up in coat and tie. "I'm hoping you're not an undercover cop."

"Think of me as a river keeper. You're having car trouble?"

"No, not at all. I was feeling a little penned in."

"Oh, I thought you might be feeling a little guilty."

"What?"

"Guilty. With all due respect, sir, your roof chicken is an incongruous monster. What were you thinking when you built one of your chicken *coops* across from a national treasure?"

"I was amazed that a property with such proximity to Roosevelt history was available. I reckoned we were providing a community service for all those hungry tourists."

"You can't see how out of place that chicken is next to FDR's house?"

"You're not a big fan of our roof chicken, are you?"

"When was the last time you went for a nature walk?"

"Can't remember. I'm an empire builder. I spend all of my time in stuffy boardrooms. Imagine a room of dreary people, nobody smiling. We only see the light of day for food."

"I want to show you something about FDR's place that you would not otherwise ever see."

"I've already taken up too much of your time," Obie said, seeming eager to leave.

"No, you've got to see this. How about tomorrow morning?"

"How far back does your family go?"

"Three hundred years-worth. Let's say 10:00 a.m. in your parking lot, under the shade of your big chicken?"

Obie smiled, "Wow, I'm having a déjà vu. Are you sure we haven't met before?"

"Destiny prevails. I'll see you at ten?" Valentine said.

"OK, if you insist."

Valentine walked back to his car.

"Hey Hollis," he said.

"What took so long?"

"Looks like I have a date."

"What's her name?"

"Destiny."

*   *   *

The next morning, Valentine made a beeline for the chicken. Obie was sitting in his mobile office talking on the telephone. Valentine tapped on the window, and Obie gave him a thumbs up. He opened the door and exited the chicken world. "I'm ready for something special," Obie said with a smile in his eye.

It was a quarter-mile point-to-point walk from roof to river. At one point, Obie stopped and took a couple of deep breaths. The conflicts of business were far away. "This fresh air is doing me good."

As they came around a turn in the bridle path, Obie saw FDR's great white house on the bluff, and off in the distance the Hudson River in deep-shadow. Obie turned his big-eyed gaze at the mysterious river for a few moments, attempting to see what Valentine saw. "Well, thank you for bringing this to my attention. My roof chicken has one hell of a view," Obie said, noticing the beauty.

Valentine rolled his eyes, turned around, and motioned for Obie to do likewise. "We're fighting a war here."

"Who are we fighting?"

"Well, folks like you," Valentine said.

"Me, I'm not fighting any war. When it comes to warfare, I'm just a chicken," Obie laughed.

"Well, let me try to put this more delicately. There's been an ongoing war between man and nature, and right now, you're part of the problem. What do you think, Obie? Look at your *thing* behind that centuries-old oak tree in the middle of the hay field."

Obie looked at his eyesore. He looked at FDR's beloved tree. Its limbs spread nearly sixty-feet wide and hung low to the ground. Obie tilted his head and squinted one eye. "Well, it's hard to argue with that tree."

"I love its aliveness," Valentine said.

"Yup, I can see that. Never really thought much about trees. To be honest, usually we just cut them down."

"Trees are the lungs of the earth. They breathe. We couldn't survive without them. They replace carbon with oxygen, the very air we breathe."

"I did not know that."

"Today, most fourth graders know this, but by the time they grow up, it will be too late."

Obie gazed at his roof chicken on the crest of the horizon. "This is not going to go over well with my board, but we need to resize that roof chicken."

"That's great. Your consciousness is expanding. Maybe big chickens are a thing of the past. I also vote that you get rid of that sign."

"Well, that chicken is brand. It used to be a much smaller roof chicken. As our marketing budget grew, that chicken just got bigger."

"Look, I'm certainly in no position to judge you for selling Chicken Charlie burgers. My family wasn't much better. Like other Yankee traders, our clipper ships brought opium from India to China. My family hooked over three million people on opium. Of course, that ended in 1849."

"That would be like me drugging sixty million people with Charlie Chicken burgers."

"Obie, what's next?"

He turned around and looked at the tree and then he looked at Valentine and then he looked back at his roof chicken. "Well, I think I've been on the wrong side of this war you mentioned. You've been telling me some wise things. I guess I have some thinking to do."

"Well, you better hurry, nature is losing this war, Obie."

CHAPTER 6

What are the chances of someone buying up the empty parking lot dinosaurs along the corridor, busting up the asphalt and reseeding with native grass?

—Valentine Hitch, *Crook's Paradise*

The next time Livy heard from Valentine it was a one-liner: "Do I have to die to get you to come back to Burleighwood?"

That question was all Livy needed to hear. His uncle's missive was enough of a kick in the butt to get him going. He donned a pair of white duck trousers and a white linen shirt, and then made arrangements for his mail, paid his bills, and extracted his blue blazer from the back of the closet, where he had shoved it when he first arrived in the Golden State. He planned to take the classic road trip on Route 66 and see what was left of America. Not to mention that it was going to take him three thousand miles to get himself in the right frame of mind to have the discussion about the fate of Burleighwood.

Livy made a quick stop at Trader Joe's in Toluca Lake to stock his car for the journey back east. "Surprise!" He imagined the priceless look on his uncle's face.

Livy headed out past Barstow on the Great Pearblossom Highway toward the Grand Canyon. By noon, he was driving across the Mojave Desert, and early that evening, he arrived at the Grand Canyon, where he found a campground and set up his tent. After dinner, sitting outside next to a fire, he looked up at the sky. Against the backdrop of a billion stars, he had a sudden longing for Burleighwood. His heart was opening. His mind went back to Jessie.

At sunrise, Livy packed his tent and gear into the back of his station wagon. He shuffled through his music collection and listened to a couple of numbers by the Beatles as he ascended thousands of feet to the alpine elevation of Flagstaff and began his descent into buffalo country. As the afternoon wore on, the air took on a cool edge. Livy started scrutinizing the eroded layers of sandstone and fossils, evidence of what the landscape looked like millions of years ago, when it was all under Paleozoic seas.

Hours later, he pulled in for the night at the Road Runner Motel. He crashed out for a while and woke up feeling that he had to get going. Livy got back on the road as the sunlight was turning the red clay into shades of pink and purple and tangerine. He went east on Route 40 and then headed north on Route 491 until he reached the Colorado Plateau and made a brief stop at the Four Corners Monument, where the states Colorado, Arizona, New Mexico, and Utah meet "in Freedom under God."

Livy spent the night at a campground in Teec Nos Pos and, the next day, made his way to Colorado Springs, then onto I-70. Later that afternoon, Livy's Volvo chugged its way up the 15-degree incline and entered the eastbound Eisenhower-Johnson Tunnel through the Continental Divide. When his wagon and mind emerged from the other end of the tunnel, a perfect crystal-blue sky set off against bright-white, snow capped mountains as far as the eye could see. Livy began the descent from the high altitude of Clear Creek County east on I-70 toward Denver. About ten miles down the interstate, he pulled off the Silver Plume exit to pee behind an abandoned dump truck. Leaving a silver plume in his wake, he flashed past something he hadn't seen in years: a hitchhiker, a well-groomed, braided millennial with his thumb extended. Livy pulled over. The hitcher grabbed the backpack at his feet and jogged toward the car. He was dressed in jeans and a Bob Dylan Budokan T-shirt. What are the chances?

Livy chuckled and rolled down his window. "Where are you headed?"

"Anywhere that gets me closer to New York works," the hitchhiker said, wiping his brow.

Before letting the lad toss his rucksack into the backseat of his wagon, Livy said, "You weren't even born when Dylan played Budokan."

"Most of the great music happened before I was born."

"Good answer, hop in."

They shook hands, the boy climbed in next the car to Livy, and off they went. "My name is Livy Hitch. What do you go by?"

"Emmett Stone."

"Nice to meet you, Emmett. There's an Igloo cooler filled with bottled water in the back of the car. Help yourself."

"Thank you, I've been dying out here."

"Don't mention it. Where are you headed in New York State?"

"The Hudson Valley."

"Guess this is your lucky day. That's where I'm headed. What are the odds?"

"Oh, that's great, I'm beginning a fellowship at Bard College."

"That's just up the river from our family place at Crum Elbow. Are you from out West?"

"I live in California. I'm a doctoral student at UC Berkeley. I'm from Palo Alto."

"What's your subject?

"I study rivers."

"Do you fly fish?"

"I don't like hooking them."

"Not even catch and release?"

"Not even. I'm really looking forward to seeing your part of the world. Isn't Crum Elbow one of the longest reaches on the Hudson?"

"You do know your rivers."

"Apparently, the Algonac Indians would make the pilgrimage to the river that flows both ways to have a good death. I guess they don't migrate anymore."

"I can't picture them coming across the country these days in an RV to die."

"You're not dying?"

"No, I'm not dying. I have some business to attend to. You like Bob?"

"I like all the Bobs—Bob Marley, Bob Dylan, Bob Weir. Although, he's more of a Bobby."

At that, Livy went off on Dylan. "Johnny's in the basement mixing up the medicine. I'm on the pavement thinking about the government."

Emmett smiled. "You sing Bob better than Bob."

I should do things like pick up hitchhikers more often, Livy mused. Emmett sure made the drive easier.

CHAPTER 7

Crum Elbow might still be a dream in some folks' heads, but you can't get there from here anymore.

—Valentine Hitch, *Crook's Paradise*

Without Hollis, Valentine reluctantly followed Crumwold's original property line until he found a breach in the twenty-five gauge wire fence. He slipped through the opening, knowing he was already way deep in over his head. Through the trees, he could see the steep slated roof of the Tower. Suddenly, he heard the downshifting of a giant truck coming up the hill from the river. He watched as a Mack heavy-hauler passed by on the new road. This was not a dirt road for launching little iceboats. It had been recently paved for heavy lifting. The question was what were they lifting? Valentine forgot all about the tower for the moment and made it by stealth to a ridge in the woods, where he finally got an open view of the shoreline. He could make out a few dark-suited figures boarding a launch. Not knowing quite what he was looking at, Valentine started shooting pictures. The speedboat, the brand-new haul-road, and the dock seemed surreal. The boat headed out into the river towards a barge being pushed by a tug. Valentine was able to zoom in and capture the faces of two men looking back in his direction. Valentine felt his old-self coming out of retirement. He hadn't scared himself like this in years.

When all went quiet, Valentine headed down the road towards the mystery. He discovered that the Rogers iceboat camp had become a way station. He started clicking photos. Then he headed back up the road from the river and ducked into the shadows of late afternoon woods, where he noticed two huge turkey vultures orbiting the tower's slate roof. Squinting into the haze, Valentine was a little surprised to see a woman walking along the path.

"Ah, a fellow trespasser," the woman said with a clear British accent and fearless smile.

"We don't get many of those out here," Valentine said, then held out his hand. "Hi, I'm Valentine Hitch," he said, not immune to the silvery blonde's staggering pulchritude.

"You're the photographer Valentine Hitch. I was going to stop by Burleighwood next. I'm Anne Rogers."

Valentine laughed, "You're related to Colonel Archibald Rogers himself?"

"He was my great-grandfather."

"He was a family friend. My Great-Uncle Humphrey and he sang together in the church choir. We're probably even related. Things get a little murky going back four or five generations."

"Not for me. I know the oral history."

"You're the genie in the *family-ology?*"

"More like a dreamer. All five Archibald Rogers called the hamlet of Crum Elbow home."

"Hamlet, now that's a word rarely applied these days."

"I get the feeling I've lived here before. It's so familiar to me."

"What took you so long?" asked Valentine, smiling.

"My grandfather convinced us that we should never go back, lest we be disappointed."

"Looks like he convinced everyone but you."

She shrugged. "I was raised in the English town of Shaftesbury. Crumwold Hall was always a faraway fantasy." She paused and nodded toward her family's famous Hall. "So how do we get inside?"

"I'm still not sure we want to end up dead," Valentine said, gesturing in the direction of another fully loaded Mack truck as it came through the back entrance to the estate and headed past them toward the river.

"My family warned me that a cult had taken control. Does that put us in danger?"

"The cult vacated the Hall when no one was looking."

"Well then, who are the new occupants?"

Suddenly, Valentine lifted his right finger to his lips and raised his other hand. A tower window opened above them. A man talking on a headset leaned his head out the window just as the Mack truck returned and rolled to a stop.

"Anne, let's continue this conversation back at Burleighwood."

Anne looked back wistfully in the direction of Crumwold Hall. "I guess I'll have to come back tomorrow."

Valentine smiled. "Gosh, you care about this place as much as I do."

"I confess, I've been obsessed for years."

"Are you parked nearby?"

"Not that far, I took the liberty of parking at the abandoned mall."

"You won't get ticketed there."

"Valentine, I'm sure glad I ran into you."

"I'm sorry you didn't get to see the inside of Crumwold Hall."

"How about we come back tomorrow morning? I don't fly out until the evening."

"Well, luckily, you've come at a very historic moment. This is my last picture show," he said, holding up his camera.

"Are you ill?"

"No, just old, too old for this."

"And this is?"

"I'm also trying to get inside Crumwold Hall, but not for sentimental reasons. For some time now I've been climbing over stonewalls and stumbling through creek beds trying to figure out what's going on in your former ancestral home …for my book."

"What kind of book?" Anne asked, looking very interested.

"Well, of course, it's a book of photography, but more of a giant op-ed piece than a picture book."

"What's the title?"

"*Crook's Paradise*," Valentine said, raising his eyebrows. "I've long thought something dark was happening here. Today my suspicions have been confirmed. Anne, I don't think this is a place you want anything to do with anymore. Thank God you ran into me and not them."

"Yes, but maybe the divine irony is that I'm actually here to protect you."

That one hit him like a small bolt of lightning. He almost fell over.

"Are you alright, Valentine?"

He smiled. "I'm just thinking."

"What's our strategy?"

"Tea?" Valentine said, then took her hand and headed toward Burleighwood. Valentine and Anne had tea in a comfortable corner of the porch, under its tall columns overlooking the Hudson. He shared his hope for Crum Elbow with another dreamer. They shared the same dream of restoration, except Valentine didn't want to stop with Crumwold Hall, he wanted to restore all of Crum Elbow.

"So how do you propose to do that?"

"With a billion-dollar bulldozer," Valentine said and laughed.

"You sound serious!"

"So do you. It's nearly dinnertime. You must be hungry from your adventures in Wonderland. I'll tell you what," Valentine smiled, "Why don't we have dinner, and afterward, I'll give you a lift over to your car. How does that sound?"

"Well, to be honest, I was planning to have some New York pizza at Mario's, but I'd be happy to forfeit that."

"Wonderful," Valentine said, then motioned to Anne. "Please join me."

They passed through a six-foot-wide set of pocket doors and at last arrived in the dining room. Anne was surprised to see a fire burning in the grate of the deep, marble fireplace. Above the mantle hung a gilded, golden eagle with a four-foot wingspan. In the center of the room sat the Regency dining table. Looking at the table, Anne noticed three place settings. "Please sit down," Valentine said, motioning to the head of the table, before disappearing into the kitchen. Anne was amazed that one of the mansions at Crum Elbow was still going. It made perfect sense to her that a man who prided himself on changing perceptions was still operating with the civility of the nineteenth century. She was in awe.

A few minutes later, Valentine returned and joined Anne to his right. Soon thereafter, Mosley entered the room from the kitchen. He was dressed in a coat and tie and looked more like a relative than a servant.

"My name is Mosley. It's nice to meet you, Ms. Rogers."

Under the smoky light of the chandelier, Mosley took drink orders and returned with two martinis and then completed the round trip to the kitchen.

"If you spend any time here, you'll find that Burleighwood's a bit otherworldly. And Mosley certainly helps keep it that way."

"Does he live here?"

"Oh, yes. He was born here. He's a charming man. He revels in being an anachronism. He's the torchbearer of Burleighwood."

Mosley returned and commented, "There was a conference of indigo buntings on the west lawn today."

"Mosley is also our resident ornithologist, Anne."

He and Valentine went back to the kitchen and returned with platters of roast beef, mashed potatoes, and green beans. "Please enjoy, Ms. Rogers."

"Please, call me Anne."

"My pleasure." Mosley dipped his fingers into a green translucent finger bowl of warm water.

Anne smiled, "I never thought I'd see those again. "

"Some things don't need to be changed," Valentine said, raising his glass. "Here's to divine intervention."

"Anne, I can see Valentine is quite smitten with you. I'm concerned about your husband," Mosley said with a wink.

"Oh, don't worry, he's properly remarried."

At the conclusion of dinner, Valentine turned to Anne. "I believe you need a ride to your car."

Hollis hadn't wanted to intrude on Valentine's impromptu date night, thus was in the kitchen rustling up his dinner when Valentine returned.

"Hollis, glad you found something to eat."

"Your lady friend ate my dinner."

"Yes, well that couldn't be helped. When one door closes, another opens."

"So, what door are you talking about?"

"As you know, Hollis, I'm very determined. When you weren't available to help me take the photographs I needed, the universe provided a lovely, blue-eyed solution."

"Where did you find this solution?"

"Well, as fortune would have it, I met my new friend quite magically in the Crumwold woods."

"Out of nowhere?"

"No doubt, out of the Crumwold Hall woodwork. She's a long-lost Rogers."

"Oh, man," Hollis said, then sat up a little straighter. "First, she eats my dinner, now …"

"And now she's helping me take your photograph first thing tomorrow. So there, Hollis," Valentine said and stuck his tongue out.

"Dang."

Once alone, Hollis reflected on the impact that Valentine had had on his life. He had no idea how much good fortune that would come from knocking on Valentine's door that fateful autumn day.

* * *

Ragtime Hollis, 1964

There hadn't been a doorbell or knocker at Burleighwood, just a strange cord hanging where a doorbell might have been and the sign: Pull Me. *Hollis pulled down on the cord releasing a cacophony of bells. A minute later, a man leaned out of the second-story window and called for him to wait. Soon, Hollis was eye to eye with his hero.*

Valentine looked to be mid-thirties. He hovered over Hollis at six feet, four inches tall with a thick, unkempt head of dark-brown hair that added another inch or two to his impressiveness.

Hollis got off to a shaky start and fumbled his words.

Valentine chuckled, "It's fine, take a few deep breaths, my friend. I've got all day."

Hollis tried to collect his thoughts. He had the bedraggled look of a starving art student. He had been a lanky six feet tall since he'd been eleven years old. The young artist was dressed in a white, short-sleeved dress shirt, a pair of black trousers, and black loafers he'd inherited from his older brother.

"Well, let me start," Valentine said. "What's your name?"

"Hollis Dixon."

"Great. Do we know each other?"

"Yes, sort of."

"Where do we 'sort of' know each other from?"

Hollis explained that he was from Franklin Corners, Mississippi, and that his family had been the subject of one of Valentine's early photographs, which Life Magazine *had published in 1954. The photograph had been part of a series chronicling social conditions in the South.*

The unembellished black-and-white picture motivated Hollis. He had carefully clipped Valentine's photograph of his family, then had it framed, and hung it on the wall next to his bed. He had brought Valentine's photograph with him when he moved to New York. It still served as his motivation whenever life got tough.

There was a pause. Valentine looked Hollis up and down. "You're a long way from home. Please come in."

"Thank you, sir," Hollis said and turned to wave off the cabbie from the train station, but his taillights were already disappearing down the drive. Now, ten years later, the ten-year-old boy "in the photograph" was sitting in Valentine's studio.

Valentine noticed a battered portfolio under Hollis's arm. "Hey, that must be your portfolio?"

"Yes, sir."

"What's your subject matter?"

"I'm still trying to figure that one out. Right now, I take pictures of just about everything."

"Well, that's the way you do it. You take thousands of photographs, and eventually, you'll find what you like and develop a voice. What do you shoot with?"

"A second-hand Rolleiflex."

"That's a classic."

"You're right, sir."

"Please, call me Valentine."

"Sorry, it's a Southern thing, sir."

"Well, we're not in the South, although this does feel like a reunion, doesn't it? Let's sit down and look at your work. Would you like a glass of lemonade, or something stronger?"

"Lemonade would be fine, thank you, sir." Hollis looked around in awe of his surroundings. He was beyond impressed that photographers could live in such opulence.

Valentine motioned to a sitting area in the corner of the studio next to the wet bar. Hollis sat down. Valentine handed him a glass of lemonade and sat down in an old-fashioned armchair opposite. Valentine began leafing through

Hollis's portfolio, pausing now and then to smile. Hollis's photographs of street scenes and people in Harlem sparked even more enthusiasm from Valentine.

"Some of these photos remind me of the work of my friend, Roy DeCarava. Are you familiar with him?"

"Yes, sir," Hollis said, then reached into his bag and showed Valentine his copy of The Sweet Flypaper of Life, written by Langston Hughes, with photographs by DeCarava.

"Good to see you've done your homework. Tell me, what's your plan? How are you surviving? New York is brutal for a young artist."

"Well, my plan is not going too well, sir. I mean, Valentine, I just got kicked out of my school today."

"Which school are we talking about?"

"The School of Visual Arts."

"Why? Your work is excellent."

"I can't pay my tuition."

"That's rubbish. There's got to be a way around that. Have you ever applied for a scholarship?"

Hollis was silent. "What scholarship?"

Valentine patted him on the back. "Well, leave it to me. Fortunately, I know exactly where to look. It's nearly dinnertime. You must be hungry. I'll tell you what," Valentine smiled. "Why don't we have dinner and, afterward, I'll drop you at the train station? How does that sound?"

"Thank you, that would be great." Hollis couldn't remember the last time he had a home-cooked meal. He inhaled what was in front of him: roast beef, Yorkshire pudding, and roasted broccoli. As they were concluding dessert, it was time to depart.

Ten minutes later, Valentine pulled to a stop in front of the train station and all eyeballs were on the car. "As you can see, it's hard to be a nobody in this car."

"Yes, I can see that. I'm so thankful to you, Valentine, really. I had no idea what to expect."

"You can come up here anytime you want. You have talent, Hollis. Don't despair. Follow your instincts. Everything will work out. Here's my card. How can I get in touch with you?"

Hollis scribbled down his phone number and handed it to Valentine, who shook his hand and then slipped an envelope into it. "You just keep believing in yourself."

When Valentine dropped Hollis off at the train station, the young man had been excited about returning to Burleighwood to work with him in the darkroom. Later that week, Valentine tried the phone number Hollis had given him, but it was disconnected. Valentine's itinerary had him scheduled to be in New York attending the Hitch Family Foundation's meeting the following Monday. Valentine was well aware of the foundation's good works but had never attended the meetings because he was always on assignment. His attendance surprised everyone, as did the complexion of the very gifted photographer he proposed for a foundation grant, but almost everyone heartily approved the grant to pay for the tuition of Valentine's charge.

Valentine hopped a cab to Twenty-Third Street in a hurry to get to the School of Visual Arts before the office closed, so he could inquire about Hollis's whereabouts. He climbed the stairs of the building just as many of the students were leaving for the day. He entered the main entrance, found the directory on the wall, and located the administration office on the fourth floor. As he waited for the elevator, out of the corner of his eye, he was surprised to spot Hollis in a janitor's uniform with a bucket and a mop. Valentine stepped back and walked over to the young man. "Hollis, I'm glad to see you're all right. I was worried about you when I didn't hear from you last weekend. When I tried to call the number you gave me, I couldn't get through."

"I'm sorry, Valentine. My phone service was turned off. It will be turned back on when I get my first paycheck. I'm really sorry."

At that moment, Bill Miller, a scrawny, red-faced man appeared and marched up to Hollis. "What have I told you about doing your work and not socializing, Mr. Dixon? I have already given you a second chance. How many chances do you think you're going to get?"

"I'm sorry, sir, I'll get back to work."

"Wait a minute, what's going on here?" Valentine demanded.

"Our Mr. Dixon doesn't understand his place here. He's no longer an aspiring photographer. He's a janitor and he'd better start behaving like one or he won't even be that."

Valentine looked to Hollis, "Give this rude little man your mop and come with me."

"But I need this job."

"No, you don't. That's what I'm here to tell you. It's all been worked out, so you'll be returning to school." With that, Valentine took the dirty mop from Hollis's hands and thrust it into Miller's. "Let this man finish your mopping. You have more important things to do and there's much to discuss about your future. Let's get you out of that outfit and get your things."

Mr. Miller stared slack-jawed as the two men headed out the front door. A colleague approached Miller holding the mop. "I see they're giving you more responsibility, Bill. By the way, do you know who that was you were just speaking with? The older gentleman?"

"I have no idea."

"Of course, you wouldn't. That's Valentine Hitch, the world-renowned Life photographer. He won the Pulitzer. We've been trying to get him to speak here for years."

"You're kidding me?"

"I kid not."

CHAPTER 8

I feel like I've been ripped, vanned and winkled but never got to sleep.

—Valentine Hitch, *Crook's Paradise*

The following morning, Valentine picked up his new friend Anne at the Motel Vanderbilt, across from the entrance to the Vanderbilt historic site. He got out and opened the door for her. She settled into the soft leather seats of the Pierce-Arrow.

Valentine smiled. "So does the motel live up to its name?"

"By virtue of proximity."

Valentine pulled onto Route 9 and headed south. "We'll start off from Burleighwood and go through the breach in the wire fence."

"I'll distract them while you get the picture."

"Let's make sure you get to experience Crumwold Hall first. If anyone confronts us, tell them your family used to live here, that should placate them."

They parked at the entrance to the carriage path that had linked the children of the neighboring estates for generations.

As they approached Crumwold Hall, Anne marveled at its appearance. "This place seems truly suspended in time. Wow, it's as if American history just came to a stop."

"Or at least gone into a kind of remission," Valentine said and led the way through the breach, but Anne's sweater snagged a little barb in the wire. Valentine turned back to free the snag. A hint of frankincense and the softness of her sweater transported Valentine. He took her by the hand and led her through the woods. As they emerged, they could see the tower in the distance, but thankfully, there was no activity. Valentine had second thoughts and warned Anne of the danger, but she wouldn't turn back. They moved quickly around to the main entrance. Valentine swung open the huge door, wincing at how loudly its iron hinges creaked. They stepped into the immensity of the entrance hall, framed by dark wood paneling from floor to ceiling. The hall had drawn its light from the enormous stone fireplace. There probably hadn't been a fire in the hearth in decades. The featherbone dance floor was enough to light up Anne's fertile imagination. She could easily imagine the familiar faces of her ancestors waltzing by.

Valentine stood lookout by the door, while Anne disappeared down the long hallway. While he waited, he noticed the hand-painted wallpaper was peeling off in large sheets from water damage. Ceiling plaster littered the floor, wiring dangled. After five minutes, Valentine started to get nervous and followed. He found Anne at the other end of the house, standing at the bottom of the stairs to the tower.

"Did you go upstairs?" she asked.

"I've been waiting at the door. I came to get you," Valentine said.

"There's someone else here. I think we should leave now."

They slipped out and circumnavigated the Hall with stealth. At the back of the house, they came upon an aluminum ladder propped up against the tower. There was also a Sprint truck, but there didn't seem to be anyone around.

"Look Valentine, the ladder is already there for you."

"I don't want to take the chance and put you in harm's way."

"Do you think you'll ever get this chance again?"

"You've got a point."

"Go take your photograph. I'll be fine. I'll hide in the woods out of sight."

Valentine, reassured for the moment, put his hands on the ladder, tested its firmness, and ascended with his camera around his neck to photograph whatever it was that was lurking. When he reached the window of the tower, Valentine positioned himself to take the photograph of the room and realized that he was photographing a man sipping a Dr. Pepper.

Grubb 3.0 spotted him, too, and threw open the window. "Who the fuck are you? You're not the Sprint guy. Give me your fucking camera." He ripped the camera from Valentine's neck, yanked out the film, and threw the camera out the window. "Now get the fuck out of here."

Valentine had had his camera shoved into his face plenty of times. He'd been pushed to the ground and kicked, but he had always managed to escape with his film. He realized he had incriminated himself. He limped down the ladder in pain, slipped on the third-to-last rung, and came crashing down onto the driveway.

Next thing, a man stood over him. "Hey, buddy, what happened to you? Are you hurt? Do you need help?"

"Oh my God, are you okay, Valentine?" Anne said, running out of the shadows.

"I think so," Valentine said, slowly getting up from the ground with some assistance from the cable guy.

"Do you want me to drive you somewhere?" he asked.

"Yes, please, we're only going next door," Anne said.

"Well, let's get you into the truck." The man helped Valentine into the cab, and Anne hopped in beside him.

"Are you feeling better?" Anne asked.

"No. Worse. He's got my whole roll of film. I knew this was a bad idea."

The driver gestured to Burleighwood's gateposts with his chin. "This your place?"

"Yes, we're so appreciative of your generosity," Anne said.

"Hey, a suggestion for you?"

"Sure," said Valentine, rubbing his knee.

"Let's put it this way, these people didn't buy this place for the river view."

"Who are *these* people?" Valentine asked.

"I don't know. I don't really want to know."

"We saw a few dump trucks," Anne said.

"The old iceboat camp lights up like Disneyland at night. But that's all I'm saying, arm yourselves."

The sound of the truck brought Tad out of his barn. Valentine always found Tad reassuring. "Pull over by that barn, please. We have it from here," Valentine said.

"I'm afraid we've taken you a little out of your way. Profuse apologies, and please know that we're warmed by your kindness," Anne said.

Tad had not had time to attach his phantom limb and came hobbling on crutches to assist. "What the hell happened to Valentine?"

"I got a little too close to what's going on next door."

"I don't know why you mess with those idiots," Tad said, shaking his head.

"Have a nice evening," the Sprint driver said, waving as he drove off.

"Well, lucky for you he came along."

"To whom do I owe the pleasure?" Anne asked.

"Tad Robbins, meet Anne Rogers," Valentine said, still wincing.

"Hi, Tad, I'm visiting from England. I'm researching my American roots."

"Lucky you, Valentine is your man, but *what* has he dragged you into?"

"When Hollis couldn't help, I had to go solo," Valentine explained. "I was very fortunate to run into Anne by the river."

"You had a surprise picnic?"

"Trust me, Tad, this surprise was no picnic," Anne said.

"The thug ripped out my film and smashed my camera. I had an entire roll devoted to crookery on the Crumwold estate."

"Oh, we're in deep shit now."

"Is Valentine in danger?" Anne asked, looking at Tad.

"They'll track the film back to Burleighwood," Tad reasoned.

"This is not good," Anne said.

"Sounds like we're *all* in deep shit," Tad said.

"No, Tad. Let's be realistic. Everybody knows I'm the freaking photographer. I'm the only one in trouble. I can't believe it's all somehow backfiring on me now."

"My driver will be coming to my motel at three to take me to JFK," Anne said. "We have plenty of time to get you fixed up. Let's get Valentine back to the house."

The celebrated Valentine Hitch, the eyes of the world, felt like a nonentity. "What the hell have I been thinking? Crum Elbow will not be returning."

*   *   *

That afternoon, after Valentine had seen his new friend Anne off at the Vanderbilt, Jessie helped him put the Pierce-Arrow to bed. She was puzzled that Valentine was putting away his treasured convertible, at a time when he would normally be out freelancing on the country roads. Valentine laid out a large industrial sheet of plastic and two long wooden planks to protect the car against the moisture of the dirt floor. He separated the planks wide enough apart to drive the car's tires onto and stationed Jessie well inside the barn. As Valentine slowly backed up the Pierce, Jessie guided him in so that all four tires were resting on the planks. He slammed the barn door shut and bolted the padlock, admitting that he didn't know when he would be using the car again, if ever.

"Are you joking?"

"I've done everything I can to save Crum Elbow. But now I have to save myself."

"Wait? What? What's going on?"

"I got in over my head next door, Jessie. In trying to get that picture of the tower, I had a bad run in with the current crop of crooks. I'm very concerned. I want to make sure that they don't bother you."

"What do you mean?"

"Let me phrase it this way. I'm really depressed. I'm exhausted. I cannot watch as everything I hold sacred is trampled and forgotten. Even just getting a picture for my book practically cost me my life. It feels like I'm not supposed to be here right now. All the signals point away."

"Leave Crum Elbow?"

"Crum Elbow is doomed."

"Whoa, slow down, Moses, don't underestimate your chosen people. You've got me, Tad, Hollis, Mosley. How about that? We've got you covered, Valentine. This is all a shock to me too, but my gut tells me that you'll be back."

"I thought Livy would have shown up by now," Valentine said.

"Well, I've been wondering for the last two years if he's going to show up."

"Don't be too hard on him. There has been a sea change in his industry."

"Meaning?"

"He regressed."

Later that afternoon, Tad stood at the barn door, waiting for the silver Mercedes to hit the speed bump in the driveway. Like clockwork, the car bottomed out and ripped the muffler off in one fell swoop. The revenge of the indigenous! The high-end Benz sounded like a stock car as the driver pulled up to the barnyard, and Tad came out.

Four doors opened at the same time, and four not-so-friendly guys, all over six feet, stepped out of the car. "What the fuck is with the road?" yelled the driver.

The lead foot went behind the car to inspect the muffler; three of his pain specialists stood mute with their arms folded. "Fuck, I think I lost my muffler."

Tad walked over and looked under the car. "Fair assessment. You know this isn't Queens Boulevard. This is a dirt farm road."

The driver glared at Tad. "Forget the muffler. I'm here to see Valentine Hitch."

"He's not here."

"Well, where is he?"

"Who are you?"

"You don't need to know. We're here to talk to Hitch."

"Well, you have to go through me."

"Who the fuck are *you*?" The menacing man stepped even closer.

"I'm Lieutenant Colonel Robbins, U.S. Marines. Let's just say I take care of Valentine."

The man realized instantly that Tad was not to be messed with. "Tell your friend we know who he is and what he's up to."

Tad watched as the message-bearer and his hit men got in the car and sped off, dragging their dead muffler. Tad knew he hadn't seen the last of them. He went back into his barn and immediately called Valentine to warn him, but the phone was busy.

Valentine had gone to his studio and noticed the answering machine light blinking on and off. Bad feelings were blinking in his gut. He pushed play. A crusty voice came on. "Tell the grease monkey and avocado girl that, thanks to you, they're lucky to still be alive. If you and any pictures you have don't disappear, they're dead meat. You don't have any idea who you're fucking with, Mr. Award-Winning Photographer."

It was suddenly painfully obvious to Valentine that he was not going gently into this good night. By early evening, he had boxed up anything Crumwold-Hall incriminating and called Tad. "I'm burning some boxes. I need your help."

"Those thugs have gotten under your skin."

"More than you might know. Now they're threatening everyone."

"I'll be right over."

Tad didn't need to ask Valentine any more questions. They lugged two boxes from his studio out to the fire pit at the bluff's edge. Tad quickly rounded up some kindling and showered the boxes with gasoline. Valentine glared into the blaze as a shower of sparks rose straight up into the stars. "I'm feeling the heat, Tad. We need to document this so they stop threatening you guys." In an unrepentant fit, he hurled a box labeled, **Crumwold Negatives** into the fire. "We'll give them one pound of flesh," Valentine said, snapping a close-up of the label before the box burst into flames.

"You're not burning your book, are you?" Tad seemed incredulous.

"The book is safe at the publisher, awaiting one last photograph."

Valentine's resentment flared up. The destruction of evidence had become funereal. He had a vision of the gilded eagle. He asked Tad to watch the fire and said he'd be right back, that he had to get hold of something. Tad looked concerned as Valentine bolted off toward the house in the moonlight.

Once he reached the dining room, Valentine looked up above the hearth and there it was, pure Americana, the golden eagle, overseeing Burleighwood like his grandfather's ghost.

Mosley came into the dining room behind him. "Valentine, is there anything I can help you with?"

Without saying a word, Valentine lifted the mighty eagle that had been there for generations off the mantle. "The time has come. My time has come," he said, then marched out of the house and back to the fire pit.

Mosley looked stunned, as if he realized his time had come, too.

Valentine returned to the bluff carrying the golden predator, with Mosley now in tow.

Tad stood up. "Really? You're going to burn family history?"

"Yup. Here's to the end of the line," Valentine said, heaving the symbol of his family's ascendency into the fire.

By now Jessie had noticed the fire and had come out to see what was going on. Valentine seemed dazed, so she turned and asked Tad if Valentine had lost his mind.

"No, it seems like he's lost his will to fight. His brain is fine."

Hollis also joined the group, watching the burning embers. "I heard you were roughed up next door. Are you okay, Valentine? What's going on?"

"It's time for the hand-off you expected, perhaps a little prematurely. My book has already upset the wrong people, and it's not even in print yet. I've put everyone in danger. I'm hoping my departure will take the heat off you."

Jessie stepped in front of Valentine. "What about the book? What exactly did you destroy?"

"All the evidence."

"What evidence? Why haven't you reported their harassment to the police?"

"I trespassed on their property, snapping photographs of things they didn't want me to see. I'm still not sure I know exactly what *is* going on."

"And this Anne Rogers lady? Where does she fit in?"

"She's offered me temporary safe harbor, and I've obliged."

"Are you telling me that this might be the last time we'll ever see you?"

"I can't answer that, Jessie, but I leave with peace in my heart knowing that Burleighwood is in good hands."

The three stood there for a moment hypnotized by the embers. They basked in Valentine's love. It felt like a funeral where the dead person was still alive. After the purge, Valentine sat alone watching the dying embers thinking about death, until a sudden revelation struck him to his feet. He dashed inside and stood before the glass-paneled case displaying silver cups and trophies won at cricket, golf, polo, tennis, and ice boating. He paused and took a hard look at his Great-Uncle Humphrey's sterling silver cricket cup. "Perfect," he said, took it with him to the fire pit, where he diligently scooped up the golden eagle's ashes, filling the silver cup to the brim. He then retired to the study and collapsed into his favorite armchair. The room was dark. The only light came from the crescent moon filtering through the window. A deep wave of relaxation came like a huge weight had been lifted, and he closed his eyes. He drifted into a dream about the days when his family used to travel between Burleighwood and New York City in a private Pullman railroad car.

*   *   *

He could hear his mother's voice in the hallway, "Valentine, you haven't even packed yet. You're always the last one!"

"I'll be there." Valentine found his suitcase and haphazardly threw together his clothes. Not wanting to be the last in the family, he hurried outside into the bright sunlight and was confronted by silence. He was surprised to find no carriage.

Having made his way to the promontory, Valentine felt reassured to see the SS Alexander Hamilton day-liner beating to windward. The gulls were laughing, and the waters were smooth. Thinking his mother had gone on ahead of him, Valentine heard the train's whistle and hurried through the allee of trees down to the railroad tracks. Hitch's private green and gold Pullman car had been attached to the back of the New York Central Line train. As the gleaming steam locomotive approached, Valentine flagged it down. The old railway porter flipped down the iron steps and ushered Valentine off to his final destination.

Valentine awakened to the sunlight streaming in his window of the study.

Two days after his departure for Shaftesbury, England, Mosley received a call from Anne Rogers to inform him of the sad news that Valentine had died of natural causes on his way to visit her. Mosley had lost his best friend. They agreed that it would be best for Anne to have Valentine cremated, as she suggested, and that his remains be shipped to Burleighwood. After some discussion, they decided to send Valentine's ashes via UPS, and that's exactly how he arrived, along with a sealed letter addressed to Mosley.

CHAPTER 9

I've witnessed in one lifetime the great cultural cheapening, where everything of value is sacrificed on the altar of convenience. Nitrogen has outpaced hydrogen. Decay has won the day.

—Valentine Hitch, *Crook's Paradise*

At the crack of dawn, Livy and his hitchhiker Emmett were through the last bit of cornfields. The highway that wound through Bear Mountain was barely wide enough for two cars. The majestic, century-old trees on opposite sides of Route 6 came together, creating a huge umbrella-like canopy. This was the thing he had missed most about the East: the beautiful trees, all kinds of trees—White Pine, Norway Spruce, Red Oak. And there it was: the New York state line.

Livy knew he was close to Burleighwood when he passed the sign depicting the profile of local hero Franklin Roosevelt, his famous cigarette holder jutting from his mouth at a forty-five degree angle. For three hundred years, change had been incremental in Crum Elbow, but now Crum Elbow itself, even after Livy's four-year hiatus, looked barely recognizable. "Seeing what's along the highways, I'm almost afraid to find out what's in the river," Livy said to Emmett.

"I'm doing my dissertation on that very subject," said Emmett. "My expertise is on zone recovery."

The word recovery set Livy off. "It looks like the whole Hudson Valley is in need of recovery."

"That's why I'm here. The model is based on consumption and growth of tax revenue. Everything is for sale, including our regulators and politicians. It's not sustainable, particularly with eight billion people on the planet."

"So, what's the answer?"

"For starters, I believe we should ban all new development. We should only be redeveloping what's already there."

"That sounds like the best solution, Emmett. Now, where am I dropping you? I'm happy to take you to Bard."

"Don't worry about it," Emmett said, smiling big. "I'll just get out here. I want to check out the river before I do anything. This is my first trip East. Thank you so much, Livy. I hope you enjoy your time with your uncle. He sounds special, him and his car."

Livy pulled over, and Emmett got out of the car, opened the back door, and retrieved his backpack. Livy also got out. He walked over to Emmett, who spoke first.

"Again, thank you for everything, Livy." They shook hands.

Livy smiled. "You've been very enlightening. It's been a joy and a pleasure. Your words are music to my ears. If you're at all representative of your generation, this country might just have a chance."

"Thank you, but the long game isn't very popular these days."

"Tell me about it! I'm only planning to be here a week, but I'll look you up the next time I'm in San Francisco."

"I have a feeling you'll be here longer."

"Excuse me?"

"The pull of the land is stronger than you think," Emmett said, shouldering his pack with a smile. And off he went.

Livy recognized a small, red, sandstone, two-foot-high tablet on the shoulder of the road in this wilderness of consumption. The ancient sandstone mileage tablet dated from the 1700s. The tablet tilted to one side like a gravestone. There were only four of those markers left in the Hudson Valley, and Livy recalled that Valentine had cared so much about this vulnerable little marker that he had it encased in stone to protect it.

Just past the mileage marker, sure enough, he spotted Burleighwood. He slowed down to make the wide arcing turn through the gateposts and headed down the long, bumpy, unpaved driveway. The familiar sound of the gravel and rocks crunching beneath the tires reminded Livy of being a child in the back seat of his parents' car. He leaned out the window and took a deep breath and immediately felt his body begin to relax after the long trip. He put his hand out the window to feel the cool country air and heard birds chirping and singing. It was nature's wall of sound. About halfway down the drive, the familiar shape of his family's ancestral home warmed his heart.

Prior to making this trip, Livy was well aware that Jessie's magic had brought the dying farm back to life. But now that he could see the results, Livy was blown away. The fields were alive with crops and vegetation, the orchards had been pruned, and the barns refurbished. He was noticing all these interesting feelings in his body. As he took in his surroundings, Livy felt the awkwardness of having not stayed in touch. He realized he hadn't been in touch with anyone, including himself.

Livy followed his realization down the driveway and around the lawn circle, where a red Jeep was parked. When she was alive, his grandmother had insisted that guests not park their cars in the circle. Margaret Hitch had never been in love with the automobile and certainly didn't want a metal contraption detracting from the classical lines and elegance of her home.

In deference to her wishes, Livy followed the drive around to the back of the house. He chose a spot overlooking the fishpond, where he and his brother, in happier days, used to fish for sunnies and search for tadpoles, frogs, and nightcrawlers. He hadn't thought fondly of his brother Archie in years. He looked up at the blue sky that was now turning a darker shade of gray, as if it were about to pour. It even smelled like it was going to rain. It rarely rained in Los Angeles, so Livy looked forward to a good eastern downpour. Livy turned off the ignition, loosened his grip on the steering wheel, and sat there for a moment thinking about Jessie. When he opened the door, Livy unknowingly popped the car out of gear with his knee. He stood outside the car, the stillness and quiet of the place relaxing him.

Livy slung his backpack over a shoulder and walked in the direction of the front door, half expecting to see the lord of the manor with one arm akimbo standing on the porch. Livy climbed the steps, pulled the long bell cord, and listened to the familiar sound echo through the house. It made him smile that it still worked. In the old days, before the Second World War, a fully liveried butler would answer, proffering a silver tray for calling cards. Livy pulled the bell cord again. There was still no answer. Remembering that his uncle never locked the door, he let himself in. All the old associations were triggered by the familiar smell of beeswax on the wood floors. The grand entrance hall had high ceilings, though very little light shone in, and its dark wood paneling made it seem gloomy, especially to a man who had spent the last twenty years at a California beach. Livy pulled back the long turkey-red draperies, revealing a galaxy of dust motes dancing in the light. After opening a window to capture the breeze off the river, he set down his bags and continued to walk through the house, calling out, "Is anyone home? Uncle Valentine? It's your long-lost nephew, Livy!"

He passed his namesake, Philip Livingston, attired in a red coat, a ruff of lace around his neck, knee breeches, silk stockings, and a powdered wig.

When Livy came to an ancestral portrait that had been banished to the far end of the hallway, a smile drew across his lips. He was face-to-face with Humphrey Hitch, Valentine's dapper and flamboyant uncle and his own great-*something* uncle. Humphrey had seemed like a character in a storybook during Livy's childhood. Great-Uncle Humphrey had been so charming in his eccentricity. One summer he convinced his fellow Hudson River neighbors that he could change the color of his eyes from brown to blue. Of course, Livy got the story second-hand from Valentine.

*   *   *

On the anointed day in 1944, cars arrived at Burleighwood and parked randomly on the grass and around the lawn circle, infuriating Valentine's mother, who was far more concerned with her perfectly manicured lawn than the color of Humphrey's eyes.

Humphrey made his grand entrance and shook hands all around. The skeptics pressed to the front. Humphrey pressed his hands against his temples and closed his eyes. After three tense minutes had passed, he reopened his eyes.

The hushed crowd leaned forward. Brown. No change. Brown. Humphrey stood unbothered. As long as he was the center of attention, he was fine with it.

Later that week, Valentine was standing at the intersection of the farm road when a familiar blue Ford Phaeton convertible pulled up in front of him in a swirl of dust. With an elbow straddling the driver's side door, out came FDR's head, complete with a Bakelite cigarette holder bouncing on his lips.

"Master Valentine Hitch. How are you this splendid afternoon?"

"Fine, Mr. President."

"So, tell me, young man, have your Uncle Humphrey's eyes changed color yet?"

"Not as far as I can tell, Mr. President. I checked at breakfast this morning. They were as brown as hash browns."

"I guess that's five dollars I'll never see again," FDR said. "If you're not too busy, might I impose on you for a great favor?"

"Certainly, sir."

"In the not-too-distant future, there's going to be a Secret Service car on my tail. When they arrive, I wonder if you would be kind enough to tell those gentlemen that I went thataway," he said, pointing at the right-hand split in the road heading north.

"I'd be pleased to help, Mr. President," Valentine said, taken aback by the war-weary face of his neighbor.

"I'm in your debt, Valentine." FDR, legs paralyzed, reached for the accelerator and off he went, left at the fork.

Minutes later, a black Secret Service car came speeding down the road. Windows rolled down, and after a quick query, they sped off in the wrong direction.

*   *   *

For old times' sake, Livy rose up on his toes and peered into Humphrey's eyes—still no change. He winked at Humphrey and made the detour up the winding back stairs to see if Valentine was in his studio in the tower. Just by the act of ascending the stairs, he felt closer to his uncle. Along the stairwell walls, Valentine had strategically positioned his deceased wife's artwork, which often served as his muse. Valentine had met his Polish wife, Paulina, in a gallery in Warsaw in the mid-sixties. Livy's aunt was a strong, independent woman. She had taught Livy how to paint and draw and encouraged a creative response to life's travails. She perished in a car accident while visiting her family in 1988, which left Valentine heartbroken. He never remarried.

Livy turned the corner and entered the studio. Valentine's pipe sat in the ashtray, waiting to be relit. Livy scanned the walls and stopped at a photograph of himself standing on a dock fishing. He must have been nine or ten years old when Valentine took the photograph. Livy's Burleighwood memories were among the happiest of his childhood. Valentine had always looked forward to Livingston's visits as much as the boy did. They spent their days hiking, swimming in the river, and identifying birds. Even the smallest things became a great adventure. Upon entering the gates, Livingston always felt liberated. He was coming from a place of judgment and comparisons and conformity. Livy retraced his steps down the creaky stairs to the first floor and headed to the kitchen. He swung open the door to find Valentine's old friend, Hollis Dixon, sitting alone at the table with a camera and a bottle of whiskey in front of him, looking as if his soul were in full debate.

Hollis looked up in disbelief. "Livingston? Is that you?"

"Yes, it's me, Hollis, but these days I go by Livy."

"Okay, I remember now. I remember your uncle trying to explain to your grandmother why you butchered such a fine old name."

"I'd contemplated calling myself Blazing Sun."

Hollis stood up, and the two men embraced. "You look great, Hollis. You haven't changed."

"Then you need glasses, my boy. Let me stand back and look at you, Livy. The last time I saw you, you were a teenager. Now you're a grown man. Sit down. Can I get you something to drink: iced tea, or I think we may have one or two bottles of cold beer?"

"A cold beer sounds great. I just got off the road. I spent five days driving across the country."

Hollis handed him a cold Michelob, and Livy practically drained the bottle in one swig. He felt his body begin to relax.

"I'm so glad you're here. I guess that explains why you didn't return any of my messages…" Hollis embraced Livy again.

"You left messages? Must've been to my landline in Malibu. I never check it. Valentine had my cell phone number. Where is my uncle?"

The smile left Hollis's face. "He's gone, Livy. Two weeks ago."

"How did it happen?"

"He was traveling from London to somewhere in the British countryside. He died of a heart attack in the sleeper car of the train."

Livy felt like the beer wasn't going to stay down. Livy put his hand over his heart. "This is not how I pictured my return to Burleighwood." He lowered his head feeling the pain.

"I understand."

The two men were silent.

"I was expecting to have dinner with my uncle, and now I'm saying goodbye."

"There he is."

"What do you mean?"

"Those are his ashes in that box in a cricket cup. As Taj Mahal would say, he be long gone like a turkey through the corn."

Livy sat his empty beer bottle down next to Valentine's remains. It didn't feel right, so he pitched the bottle into the trash and asked if there had been a burial.

"Your uncle broke with your tradition and chose not to be buried with his family. He wanted to be cremated and have his ashes scattered on the bluff overlooking the Hudson river as the sun goes down. He told me he felt a much stronger connection to the land than he did the churchyard."

"I need a little time alone."

"I understand. Take your old room on the second floor."

When Livy walked across his room, the creaky eighteenth-century floorboards creaked above him. Livy had taken his old room. The bed was all set up for him; for four years it had awaited him. Livy dried off after a shower, dressed, and sat at the edge of the bed trying to wrap his mind around the fact that Valentine was dead. Livy knew he would kick himself forever for not coming back East sooner. He could hear rain on the roof. He emerged from his room and headed down the stairs, closing the window he'd opened as he passed it in the corridor, on the way to the study. Most of the rooms hadn't changed at all since his grandmother died.

When Livy appeared in a black T-shirt and blue jeans at the door of the study, Hollis stood up. Livy felt as if he were seeing Valentine's ghost. "Hey, what's the deal with the coat and tie?" Livy asked, feeling sartorially challenged as he stepped over the polar bear skins that had been strewn across the floor by some long-dead ancestor.

"I'm often confused with the head waiter these days."

"Huh? Really?"

"Wearing a tie makes me feel closer to Valentine."

"Well, that's got to be a good feeling," Livy said.

"Maybe it's destiny. Maybe he had to go before you showed up."

"Trying to make me feel better? I thought you were a photographer, not a philosopher."

"Sometimes it takes a thousand words to understand the big picture."

Livy spotted Valentine's Zippo lighter sitting on the curly-maple secretary. He could still recall the sound of his uncle's periodic flicking of flint and lighting his pipe.

Mosley's entrance snapped him back to reality. "I'm sorry this all happened so fast, and you didn't get to see your uncle before he passed."

"Thank you, Mosley. How are you? We're all family here."

"I'm not sure I'm ready to talk about Valentine. What kind of a drink can I get you?"

"Oh, that's fine Mosley. I can get my own drink."

"As you wish, but after a long journey and such sad news, I insist on taking care of you. What would you like?"

"Well, if you put it like that, be my guest. This room screams of scotch to me. Neat, please."

Livy's body sank into the bottomlessness of the armchair while his mind continued to float. The ancient one returned with the drinks.

"Thank you, Mosley," Livy sighed.

Mosley handed Hollis something that looked like a lemonade spritzer. "Aren't you going to have something stronger, Hollis?"

"Any stronger and I won't be here much longer. I gave your uncle my word when I moved in that I would stop drinking. When we lost Valentine, I almost caved. Then you came along, Livy, and here we are."

Mosley stood before them. "It's very comforting to have you here, Livy."

"I feel the same way about you, Mosley."

After Mosley departed, Livy turned to Hollis. "I'm concerned about Mosley."

"Valentine's death hit him hard," Hollis said as he handed Livy a square envelope addressed to Valentine, with the Saint James school emblem. "Didn't you go to Saint James?"

"Hook, line, and sinker. There wasn't really a choice." Livy opened the envelope and looked over the invitation to a fundraiser for the school to be held in New York City. He saw a familiar name on the committee, Archibald Putnam Hitch, his estranged, older brother. Growing up, Archie took out all his angst and frustration on Livy. It was the same old hand-me-downs from his father and his father's father. They had been born into a genetic gulag. They got the 'gu' from their mother and the 'lag' from their father. Livy looked at the mid-July date and started thinking. He had a sudden yearning for connection with his older brother.

Their conversation was interrupted by a crack of thunder and a big gust of wind that blew the branches of the tree just outside the study against the window. Livy and Hollis sat quietly listening to the rain batter the old hand blown-glass.

The rumbling sky took Livy's mind across the river, high up in the Catskill Mountains—the full impact of Valentine's death hit him in that moment.

"We may be in for one," Hollis said.

"Excuse me?" Livy asked.

"They're predicting flash flooding. I hope your car windows are rolled up."

Had he rolled them up? Livy poured his glass of scotch into his enormous emptiness. His eyes traveled up the wall, and he pointed to the blank space above the couch. He could see the dark rectangle where the painting once hung. When The Spanish Dancer went to New York, Burleighwood was reborn.

At that moment, nature spoke with thunderous applause. "Oh my God, my car!" Livy rushed out the back door and down the steps in the pouring rain. Hollis grabbed Valentine's jumbo black and orange umbrella and chased after the now-soaked Livy. When they reached the embankment, Livy's eyes darted around looking for his car. It was nowhere to be seen. Had the universe eaten it, swallowed it whole? Then, farther down the hill, he could make out through the opaque light the outline of something square and large sinking into the pond. On closer inspection, it was indeed his past.

Livy skidded down the embankment as his beloved Volvo sank into the fishpond. By the time he got to the shore, all that was visible was his solar-yellow mountain bike attached to the roof. Livy's life was in that car: his laptop, his music, his camera, all those pictures from the Grand Canyon, that picture of his ex-girlfriend, Leslie (the one that still saddened him every time he looked at it), his address book with names and phone numbers of old friends going back to before boarding school. His blue blazer had also gone down with the car. As Livy helplessly paced along the pond's edge, Hollis followed him with the umbrella. Hollis phoned Tad. Instead of Tad, they heard the steady pulse of a tractor climbing up the road from the river.

"Here comes Jessie on her John Deere."

At that moment, Jessie in rain gear appeared on her tractor. It had been repainted with sunflowers, and a bright yellow tractor umbrella protected her from the elements. She glanced down at Livy and smiled, "Hey, California."

Wrapped in a camouflage hooded rain poncho, Tad interrupted the reunion and directed Jessie as she backed the tractor to the edge of the pond.

Livy looked at Hollis, who raised his eyebrows in agreement. "Who is that guy?"

"He's your uncle's caretaker. His name is Tad Robbins. He's a mechanical prodigy."

Jessie released the winch, and Tad grabbed the cable heading toward the water.

At that moment, Livy noticed that Tad had a prosthetic leg. "Wait a minute, let me do that. It's my car after all," Livy said, then grabbed the towing cable and waded out to his car.

When Livy hooked the winch line to the bumper, Tad called out. "Not on the bumper, you'll yank it right off. Hook it to the undercarriage."

Livy reached under the water groping until he found a solid hookup under the chassis.

"Good job, Livy," Jessie said, as she turned on the winch. Livy, soaked to the bone, watched as she slowly dragged what remained of his past out of the pond, up the hill, and onto higher ground next to the house.

"Tough luck, man," Tad said. "We had flash flood conditions. You must have popped it out of gear and forgot to put the emergency brake on. Do you want your bike before Jessie tows the car to my shop?"

"Please, I'm going to need it. By the way, I don't think I've had the pleasure," Livy said, extending his hand to Tad.

"Oh, I'm sorry. Tad, meet Livy Hitch, Valentine's nephew," Hollis said.

Tad nodded. "So, you're the new Lord of the Manor? A tough act to follow. Place will never be the same."

Livy gazed at the vision of shapeliness sitting on the John Deere, drew in a deep breath and died a thousand deaths.

Jessie cut the engine, hopped off the tractor, and stuck the landing as if she were Cat Woman. She was dressed to the nines in her red wellies. When Livy headed in her direction, she reached out and lightly grasped Livy's hand. "I'm sorry you didn't get a chance to see Valentine."

Livy nodded. "Thank you."

The rain came steadily down. "Time for a cup of tea by a warm fire, and, Livy, you could use a hot shower," Jessie said.

"I'm down with that," Livy said. He'd been expecting a cold shoulder, but instead, something warm and wonderful traveled up his arm and into his head. Livy couldn't quite believe it.

"Join us, Tad?" Jessie asked.

"I have stuff to do. Tea isn't my cup of tea." Tad said. Without saying anything more, Tad went to the barn and pulled out Valentine's touring car, so Livy wouldn't be stranded.

After Livy showered and changed, he, Jessie, and Hollis settled in with their cups of tea before a birch log fire with its crackling bark.

Livy sat there brooding. "What did Tad mean by calling me the Lord of the Manor."

"This place is yours, Livy. Valentine left everything to you," Hollis said.

"The whole place?"

"You got it. The whole place," Hollis said.

"Debt and all?"

"Well, thanks to The Spanish Dancer, it's all been paid off. Valentine saw to that."

"Well, I'll be damned! Is there anything left to cover maintenance and taxes?"

"For about a year," Hollis said.

"Then what?"

"A year gives you enough time to figure all this out," Hollis said.

"Listen, guys, I can already tell you the answer."

Hollis read the museum of Livy's soul. "Tell us in a year."

"There's no way. It's just not doable. I can't afford the luxury of a primeval forest. I live in a condo in California. I'm a struggling voiceover artist."

"What are you *feeling* for this place?" Jessie asked.

"I have a lot of feelings for this place, Jessie."

"Valentine told me that you would know exactly what to do when the time came to decide the fate of Burleighwood," Jessie said.

"I don't know anything about real estate."

"This ain't real estate. He knew what he was doing, picking you. You just need to act," Jessie said.

Livy gazed back into the fire. "Maybe after I dry off from the baptism."

CHAPTER 10

Our whole culture shifted during my lifetime. We developed the antidote for everything but greed.

—Valentine Hitch, *Crook's Paradise*

The next morning, Livy awakened to the rattle of teacups. He sat up in bed while the traces of his dream were still there; then the dream faded out. He had burned some white sage that he had picked up at the Navajo exchange in Gallup before he went into dreamtime. The smoky scent of sage gave way to a loamy river breeze. As he climbed out of bed, Livy noticed the mini red Nerf football in a swirl of dust under the chest of drawers. Clearly, Valentine's vacuum rarely made it to the second floor.

That little red ball came with a lot of feelings and memories of happier times. Back when he and his brother still spoke.

About an hour later, Livy made his way down the stairs and stopped in the dining room. The golden eagle on the mantle that had been hanging there since Revolutionary times had vanished. When Livy reached the kitchen door, Mosley was sitting in his spot at the outsized, rustic oak farm table, which had taken a small crew of able-bodied men to put into position a century ago. It had not been moved since. But where was the gilded eagle?

A rustic wooden bench and assorted chairs flanked the table. Mosley stopped reading the newspaper and rose from his seat ready to serve.

"Welcome home, Livy. Will you take your breakfast in the dining room?"

"Thank you, Mosley. The kitchen is fine."

"Do you still drink coffee?"

"Yes, please, Mosley. Something smells great. What's for breakfast?"

"We're still in the industrial age here. Think eggs benny, smoked Canadian bacon, maple syrup, and tomato juice."

"I haven't had a breakfast like that since the last time I was here."

"You know, Jessie has been trying to raise consciousness around here, but she hasn't really infiltrated the main house yet. But I did notice goat's milk in the refrigerator."

While Mosley served breakfast, Livy started thinking about his night with Jessie and Valentine. "How is Jessie?"

"Oh, she's certainly a ray of light here. Valentine and I thought you two might be an item."

"So how *are* things, Mosley?"

"At this moment I'm getting you a tomato juice. Then I'm going to pack."

"Pack? Where are you going?"

"All my life I have wanted to go to Europe. The family went off to Europe without me. It's finally my turn."

"Sounds like it will be good for you to get away from Burleighwood and see the rest of the world."

"Yes, that's what scares me. I preferred the days when the world came to Crum Elbow."

"Do you need a ride to the airport?"

"No, I have a car coming."

"Vacation?"

"Of sorts."

"You're coming back, right?"

"I guess that depends on what happens to Burleighwood now that Valentine isn't here to protect it."

"Sounds like you don't trust me to do the right thing."

"I realize money matters, Livy. I don't wish to add to your pressure."

Livy nodded in appreciation. "Are we talking London, Paris, Switzerland?"

"First stop, London. Then the English Countryside."

"That sounds like something you would do."

"Yes, I'm really a country gentleman at heart."

After his breakfast, Livy received a telephone call from his uncle's lawyer, the executor of the estate, Tom Pollack. Looking for some sort of commitment from Livy, he scheduled a meeting for them that morning. Livy set out for the lawyer's office ten minutes too late. Thanks to Tad, Livy barreled around the lawn circle in Valentine's Pierce-Arrow and headed down the driveway hoping to make up time. It felt strange to be in the car without Valentine. Livy had always ridden shotgun. The old car was like time travel. Valentine used to cruise along the winding country roads at breakneck speeds while telling fantastic stories. Livy dearly missed the conversation and camaraderie. He missed Valentine's commentary on life.

Livy rounded the corner and slammed on the brakes, just in time to avoid smashing into the large, neon-orange triangle on the back of Jessie's tractor. He followed behind, patiently waiting for the first opportunity to blast past the slow-moving tractor with its fine-looking driver. As the drive widened, Livy saw his opportunity to pass. He hit the accelerator only to jam on the brakes again, as Jessie swerved to block his passage.

"What's your freaking deal," Livy sputtered and had to wait to pass until they finally reached the back-farm gate, where Jessie made a wide swath of a turn and gunned her tractor down the lane to greener pastures before the barbed wire. He noticed that she never looked back. She was letting the tractor do the talking. Burleighwood was the one subject too charged for words.

Livy arrived at the offices of Livingston & Webb, located in the former Masonic Lodge, which had four imposing marble Greek columns at the entrance. Before the Second World War, Crum Elbow had been predominantly Protestant, and the lodge had anchored the town's culture.

Mr. Pollack's office was a holdover from the decades when everything was made of dark wood. The oak paneling, the richly grained mahogany partners desks, and the bookshelves, too, were all a rich brown.

Tom Pollack introduced himself to Livy. "Shall I call you Livingston or Livy?"

"Livy, please."

"Livy, it is," he said, looking up from the will and over his bifocals starting to form an opinion about Livy. Pollack went on to recite each of Valentine's intentions. Not surprisingly, Valentine had thought through every detail carefully. The land was now safe from the nefarious hands of developers. The bequest included nearly five hundred acres of wooded riverside parkland. Valentine's generous gift would help complete the last link in the Emerald Necklace, which included protection for huge tracts of undeveloped land along the Hudson, for eternity.

"Valentine was a firm believer that family was *where you found it*. He had carefully handpicked those whom he envisioned as the final generation to occupy Burleighwood. It was Valentine's noble intention to grant a life estate to everyone currently living on the property, with the stipulation that the land would pass to The Green Borders Conversancy when the last one of the Burleighwood gang died or moved away. Tad could live and work on cars out of his barn. Hollis was granted life occupancy of the main house and his studio. Jessica could stay on the farm and reside in her river house."

"What about Mosley?"

"Your uncle did make special provisions for you and Mosley, Livy. Valentine has set up a trust for Mosley. Of course, he ultimately left this all up to you, which others may not know."

"The house and two-hundred acres of land are deeded to you, and Valentine left enough funds to take care of it, at least for the next two years."

"My life is in Los Angeles," Livy said, shrugging his shoulders. "I'm planning to put the house on the market before I head home in two weeks."

"Perhaps Valentine overestimated your devotion to Burleighwood. He was extremely specific about his plans. He always assumed you were on board. He left you the funding, a working farm, and a family to boot."

"But I've never wanted to live here," Livy countered. "Valentine knew that, or at least I thought he did, and *now* I find out that the estate comes with a commune? What was Valentine thinking of saddling me with all these people?"

Pollack flipped through the pages of the will. "Well, in the end these were his intentions, but he left you an out. Legally you have ultimate jurisdiction. You can pull the plug on the whole thing. I already have a potential buyer, Dr. Emerson Winks, the director of the newest Roosevelt historic site. Money is not the problem, he seems to have Mrs. Van Rensselaer wrapped around his finger, which is good because he's not only interested in the house, he wants to save Crum Elbow."

"What does he want our place for?"

"Burleighwood is the last remaining historic house in private hands at Crum Elbow, not the town, of course, but the historic turn in the river. His dream is to repurpose your family's estate into a welcome center. You know, as much as he is a crazy control freak, I almost have to concede him at this point. His dream is more than just a green-bordered river from Troy to Yonkers. More than just fixing up an historic house, Winks's vision is to restore the continuity of the landscape FDR loved: from the ancient trees down to Hudson River Woodchucks."

"What about the mall in between?"

"Winks now owns it. He bought the mall out of receivership. He's going to bulldoze the complex this Saturday. But that's a story for another time. You have more important things to think about. The sooner the better, Livy. There are no restrictions on you. You're free to sell the house and the grounds. I know that Winks is interested in the entire property. It's all up to you. Grace period and all. You should talk to Fifi Hoffmann."

"Who's that?"

"She's a local real estate broker. Fifi knew your uncle. The last time Valentine thought of putting the place on the market, he worked with her."

Livy rued the day that Valentine passed away. He was at the end of the line. Livy left the lawyer, descended the cold marble steps, looked both ways, then navigated his way across Market Street and in through the doors of Henderson & Livingston Realty. As Livy entered, he was met by a horsey woman wearing red reading glasses on a neck chain.

"I'm here to see Ms. Hoffmann," Livy explained.

"I'm Fifi Hoffmann."

"I'm Livy Hitch."

"Nice to meet you, Mr. Hitch. You must be the nephew. Coffee?"

Livy looked across the desk at all of Fifi's pictures: Dalmatians and granddaughters. "No, I'm fine." Livy was in no mood for small talk.

"Please sit down," she said, gesturing to the chair across from her desk.

"Thank you," Livy grunted and sat down in a low-level brain fog. "I'm here to possibly sell your Burleighwood estate. The lawyer-friend Tom Pollack sent me over here. He told me you previously listed the property before."

"That was back when Valentine thought he might be forced to sell the entire estate. But the painting changed all that," she said. Then, she tilted her head in the other direction. "Of course, I was happy it worked out for Valentine."

"What's the current market price of the whole estate?"

"Well, there's not much value in the house, the buyer might opt to tear it down. The value is in the land, as you can imagine. Everyone in our business has their eye on Burleighwood. It's the last of its kind. Our brokers refer to it as *Burleighworld*."

"Let's see what we can get for the whole thing."

"You're reading my mind. How long do you plan to be here?"

"Not long, but I assume we can continue working this out over the phone, if necessary?"

"Of course, we can communicate any way you like. As you might expect, we require a six-month exclusive?"

"Sure."

"We'll want to put up signs as soon as possible."

"Is that necessary?" Livy said, anticipating blowback from the extended Burleighwood *family*.

"Some of my best customers drive-by and drive-in. The new owner could be driving by right now. Trust me, this is how it works. Let me do my job."

Livy had no idea she already had two buyers lined up for a secret bidding war—Emerson Winks versus Homer Junior. Parkland versus plenty of parking.

The battle was on.

Mosley was up early the next morning to take a final walk. He visited three favorite spots that he might never see again.

First, he hiked down to the shoreline to say goodbye to the marsh herons. Then he aimed his binoculars across the river, where he could just make out Riverby, which had once been the house of the great naturalist John Burroughs. In fact, it took Mosley's keen eye to identify Burrough's rooftop hidden amid the trees. Mosley continued on from the river to his raptor lookout on the bluff. Then, he walked across rutted fields listening to the *symphony* of the day. When he was a boy, Valentine had recognized that Mosley possessed a supernatural power. He had ears from heaven. Mosley could listen in different directions and identify all the feathered musicians. Today, he singled out the *here, here, here* of the Tufted Titmouse. The *pinging* of the Field Sparrow. The *tea-kettling* of the Carolina Wren. The *slow sawing* of the Great Crested Flycatcher. Then he went farther afield to find his friend the Red-Tailed Hawk that frequented the abandoned tower left over from the days of pheasant shooting at Burleighwood. He raised his binoculars, and he saw Jessie as she came over the horizon at the wheel of her tractor. Mosley waved for her attention.

Jessie brought the tractor to a halt, cut the engine and, looking down at Mosley, dismounted it. "Did you change your mind, or is this our final goodbye?"

"No, I'm on my way. I was saying goodbye to my friends."

"Remember, you promised to call me when you land at Heathrow."

"I gave my word."

"I'm worried about you going off into the unknown. We're going to miss you."

"I'm going to miss everyone and everything about this place. I spent my whole life here, nearly eighty years." He paused, raising his eyebrows. "Time for new. I'm looking forward to seeing birds I've never seen."

Jessie smiled, "I can't argue with that. You have my permission. I'm just selfish...I don't want to see you go. I'll miss you too much." Jessie stepped forward and wrapped her arms around Mosley to send him off with a kiss on the forehead, which was perfect for Mosley.

Livy was arriving back on the property as Mosley's black town car was making its egress through the gateposts. Mosley simply waved to Livy. Livy watched as the black limo paused at the lip of Route 9 then turned south toward Poughkeepsie.

About two miles down Teller's Hill, suddenly, Mosley was in an alien world. Everything had changed. His first reaction was to lean forward to ask the driver to turn around. But then Mosley leaned back and closed his eyes. Too late. Invisible forces were in motion.

One thousand feet above Burleighwood, Commander Winks, wearing blue-tinted aviator goggles, completed his first arc over the Hudson. To the south, he could see miles down beyond Newburg Bay to where the river narrowed and was flanked on either side by the Hudson River Highlands. One of the mountain peaks had been named after Anthony Hogan, a pre-Revolutionary war ship captain whose good-natured crew thought the rocky peak resembled their leader's prominent proboscis. Henceforth, this peak was known as Anthony's Nose. Winks completed the arc and pointed the plane back toward Crum Elbow. As Winks banked, he could see Burleighwood from the cockpit, an emerald oasis embedded in the lurching sprawl.

Livy had been practicing yoga by the river, where he looked up and noticed a yellow seaplane, watching as it completed a full circle above the property. Later that afternoon, Livy headed down the dirt road flanked by a rustic, wooden fence. A mixed flock of starlings and mockers landed in the tilled field. Two turkey vultures were resting on the roof of the dilapidated dog kennel. He heard the suddenness of the Purple Martin and marveled at how much he remembered from his bird rambles with Valentine.

Then, in the distance, Livy spotted the weather-beaten barn.

Tad's mechanical laboratory. Peering into the barn, Livy saw several big red-metal Craftsman tool chests on wheels with rows of all sizes of sockets and shelves of ratchets and wrenches. There were generators and air pumps and jars of bolts. The earthy reek of animals and hay and soil was mixed with the sharper smells of gasoline, solvents, and grease. Clearly, Tad kept the large barn doors wide open so he could breathe. Livy tiptoed around pools of oil and an obstacle course of old parts and tires.

"Hello, Tad. You alive?"

"Under here," came a muffled reply. All Livy could see was one black, steel-toed boot sticking out from underneath the car. Tad had taken off his prosthetic leg and set it in the front seat.

Tad rolled out from underneath the car, looked up at Livy, and exploded in anger. "I saw Fifi pounding her sign in this morning. You? You're selling out Valentine?"

"Valentine sold himself out," Livy said, bristling, then promptly changing the subject. "What's the deal with my car?"

"Still not dry. Maybe tomorrow or the next day."

"Do you think it can get me back to California?"

"Pennsylvania if you're lucky. California if we are."

Hollis pulled up in his Jeep with Jessie. "Hello, Livy," he greeted, somewhat cheerfully.

Jessie, however, glowered. "The prodigal nephew has returned to sell out the ancestral home," Jessie said.

"You mean Benedict frickin' Arnold," Tad said with a full-bile grumble.

"Ah, what's up Tractor Woman?" Livy asked.

"I guess I owe you lunch." Jessie must have realized after the fact that, even though she had gotten some pleasure out of it, blocking Livy's way to the lawyer's office with her tractor had been juvenile.

"Hollis and I were just talking about the future," Jessie said. "I don't get it, Livy. I would think Valentine's most creative nephew would feel a profound connection to this place, but you seem indifferent. What happened?"

"I'm not indifferent. This is financial not emotional."

"You were the only person in the family Valentine felt he could trust *not* to sell out Burleighwood. He never forgave your father for selling the north pasture so the Grubb's could build that godforsaken mall. He thought that the rest of your family were a bunch of piranhas," Hollis said.

Livy sighed. "As much as Valentine wanted the living arrangements to remain the same, he was unrealistic to think I could take over this place."

"He trusted your *integrity*," Hollis said. "I'm sure Valentine spoke with you about his book project."

"Oh, the one he's been slow cooking on the back griddle for forty years now. I guess I'd know if he'd finished it."

"He was putting the finishing touches on it when he died. He photographed things he shouldn't have next door," Hollis said. "That's why he had to bail."

"Yup, there is some weird shit going on over there," Tad confirmed.

"What kind of shit? What are we dealing with?" Livy asked.

"You need to see the photos." Hollis said.

"Well, okay then, let's all go have a look." Livy nodded.

The foursome approached Burleighwood's nineteenth-century stone creamery. "You work here?" Livy asked Hollis in disbelief. "This place used to be crawling with copperhead snakes."

"It's my studio now," Hollis explained. "Welcome to Soho on the Hudson." Hollis opened the doublewide Doubleday doors and flipped on the lights.

Livy soon forgot about the snakes of his past and was drawn to the rear wall, which was covered from floor to ceiling with black-and-white photos of heroes of the Civil Rights movement: Malcolm X, Rosa Parks, Martin Luther King, and Elijah Muhammad, among others. This reminded Livy that Hollis was a big deal in the outside world.

Hollis motioned them over to his long, oak worktable. The entire surface was covered with Valentine's manuscript.

Livy walked over and picked up a photograph of the invasion of the minivans, the Hudson Valley's very own Pearl Harbor. The shot had been taken from the window on the way up the stairs to Valentine's studio. It showed the ugly tar-covered roof of the neighboring mall, with the huge HVAC units that had been airlifted onto it.

Hollis burrowed through his pile and found the picture that almost killed Valentine. "This is it," he said, placing it under a lamp, and all four gathered around.

"What's that foamy shit dripping off the dump truck?" Livy asked.

"I don't know, Livy, but it looks toxic." Hollis said.

"This probably should have been left alone. But you know Valentine once he captures fire," Jessie said. "He was convinced that some nefarious operation was being run from the tower right next door. He had reached the top of the ladder outside the window, aimed his camera, and adjusted the focus. The next thing he knew, his camera hit the gravel. Then, the same thing happened to him. He had been deliberately pushed off the ladder."

"Chasing down that picture of the tower almost killed him, matter of fact, it probably did kill him. It turns out your uncle was on a collision course with local corruption. He tried to involve me in taking that picture," Hollis said.

"These are definitely scary people. I'm now nervous about going out in the fields alone," Jessie said.

"Why didn't somebody press charges? My uncle was obviously assaulted. *Who* are these people?"

"All I know is that they are next door and better stay there," Tad said, on a one-limbed war footing.

"I guess I don't have to ask if you're armed," Livy asked.

Tad smiled at Livy. "To the teeth."

"How many teeth we talking?"

"A big smile's worth."

Hollis looked to Livy. "These are bad people, and Valentine knew it, Liv. He warned me that they were above the law, part of a two-tiered justice system. Right before he bailed, Valentine threw the gilded eagle over the mantle into the fire."

"I was going to ask you about that," Livy said.

"He thought it was over," Hollis said.

"What?" Livy asked.

"Crum Elbow, Burleighwood. Valentine pulled the ripcord."

"Can't say I knew this part of my uncle," Livy said, feeling bewildered, looking to Jessie for answers.

"He left Crum Elbow to take the heat off of us. But to answer your question, Livy, I think Valentine threw the eagle in the fire of finality. He never expected to return."

"Yeah, okay, that sounds more like Valentine," Livy said.

CHAPTER 11

Nothing but dead air has filled the vacuum that followed Franklin Roosevelt's last fireside chat.

—Valentine Hitch, *Crook's Paradise*

The following morning, Livy hopped on his mountain bike and headed out the driveway with new resolve. The driveway was a rough ride of shifty gravel. He made a left on Route 9, headed north for less than a mile, then made a hard left into the recent history of Manor Drive. Once beyond the one-family ranches with ancient oaks in their back and front yards, Livy saw the Hudson through the trees. He descended past the white fences down to the shore landing. He eased on the brakes at the bottom of the hill, where he could see the red-roofed railroad station, a Roosevelt-era time capsule on the Hudson. From his uncle's stories, he could easily imagine the all-upper-body FDR detraining at Crum Elbow.

Livy began tracing the abandoned tracks along the river and soon located the overgrown entrance to the carriage trails of Crumwold estate. The land was threaded by a fifteen-mile network of meandering dirt carriage trails barely wide enough for one car. Livy plowed through the thicket and hit the brakes as he crossed a small, rickety wooden bridge that spanned Crum Elbow Creek. He followed his curiosity deep into suspicious territory and sinister trees. His tires sunk into the mulch of leaves, moss, mildew, and chicken mushrooms. It was just him, his bike, and the steep hill rising in front of him like Valentine's expectations. Livy approached his nefarious neighbors from the backwoods to get a good look at what was going on for himself.

At the top of the Crumwold knoll, Livy looked out in disbelief at the vast clear-cut. Colonel Rogers's favorite trees had been ripped from the soil. The land had been scorched, habitats and all. It looked like a bombed-out wasteland. Livy could make out the estate's abundance of towers and stone geometries through the trees. His gaze settled on the red-tiled roof of the tower room. He thought of Valentine, who had spent his life taking pictures that set the record straight. He thought of Valentine on the ladder and that one last picture that had backfired.

Further afield, Livy spotted a man standing in the flatbed of a silver Dodge Ram pickup truck looking through the site of a gun. Suddenly feeling more trespasser than indignant, he jumped back on his bike and crouched low, swerving deliberately to avoid being sniped. Once out of sight, he stood up on the pedals and, as if he were on skis, slalomed down the rest of the hill. At the bottom, he merged with a single-track trail that dumped him into a dry creek bed and then bounced his way through the final stretch of the woods. The route finally spilled him out where the railroad tracks crossed Crum Elbow Creek. Once across, he peddled his way back up the steep River Road toward Burleighwood.

Just when he was about to make the arc into the safe confines of Burleighwood, Livy heard a squeal of wheels behind him and quickly looked to his left as the silver Dodge Ram pickup truck bore down and sideswiped him off the bike. He flew through the air in free fall from the bike and crashed into the bushes as the bike continued over his head and landed in the drainage ditch. Livy lay there in the arms of the honeysuckles. His shoulder hit first and was sore but functioning. His neck seemed to be fine. A feeling of gratitude rippled through his body. Then he noticed the remains of Valentine's treasured route tablet shattered to pieces. He picked himself up and out of the bushes and started gathering the shards of red sandstone with the fantasy of gluing them back together.

Jessie pulled up beside Livy in her Ford pickup truck. She leaned out the window and could see the look of distress on Livy's face, "What on earth happened to you?"

"I just got sideswiped."

"Any broken bones? Do you need a doctor?"

"No, just still in shock. I think one of our whack-job neighbors just tried to kill me with his truck."

"But you're not hurt?"

"No, the bushes broke my fall. I'm lucky, but Valentine's mileage marker wasn't so lucky. I can't just leave it. Do you have a box?"

Jessie grabbed a burlap bag from the back of her truck and hurried over to help him gather the fragments of sandstone. Livy carefully put the shards in the bag, as if he planned to glue them back together. It was like he was holding pieces of the family china. When all the fragments were rescued, Livy carefully placed the bag in the truck, and Jessie walked over to the ditch, picked up the bent bike, and loaded it, too. She looked Livy over. "Do you need help getting in the truck?"

"No, I'm fine, thanks for all your help, Jessie."

They got in her truck and soon headed down the driveway. "What the hell am I thinking?" Livy said. "I could be surfing right now. I'd probably be safer with the sharks."

Driving by the *For-Sale* sign hit Jessie like a punch in the gut. She looked at Livy in disbelief.

"There is already an offer," Livy said.

"Should I laugh or cry?"

"Coming from this bloke Emerson Winks."

"Not surprised. He has the agenda and the financial backers. It's hard enough being here without Valentine. But selling Burleighwood would be too painful. I couldn't be here for that," Jessie said.

Livy paused. "I understand how you feel."

"It seems like this place is going down in flames." Jessie eased the truck around the lawn circle and came to a stop. "Do you need help getting inside?"

"My legs are fine. It's my right shoulder."

"You need to ice it immediately."

Jessie helped Livy extract his bike from the truck bed. Then Livy retrieved the remains of the mileage markers.

"What are you planning to do with those?"

"My family have been hoarders for generations. Instead of having horses in our stables, we have stuff. I'm sure there's a spot for these."

The next morning, Livy stood at the entrance of the horseless stable carrying the shards of Valentine's broken world. He had attached a tag to the burlap: FRAGILE, *Colonial remnants (Possible home: New York Historical Society, gift from Valentine Hitch)*. Livy was addressing future generations tasked with making sense of the contents of the bag. He looked for a spot to store his precious cargo, a place that would be easy to find. He spotted a shelf high above the bones of his family history. Once Valentine's beloved markers had been safely stored on the upper shelf, Livy looked around at the attic of his life.

The world was made of stories, and they were stacked to the rafters in front of him. Many of the stories would remain a mystery to anyone. He admired the proud Edwardian furniture. He noticed that his old wooden hobbyhorse, the most ancient of toys, seemed tiny to him now. He could imagine himself three feet tall. He could feel his mother standing over him while he rocked on the hobbyhorse. His hovering mother with her alcohol breath. He let out a groan. At that moment, the whole room felt like a storehouse of pain. The smell of old wooden toys reminded Livy of happier days. He found his father's tackle box from their fishing trips in Quebec. His mother's picnic basket reminded him of the days when he and his brother still did things together. He rummaged through a trove of memories from the past: metal Christmas tree stands, his brother's pogo stick, and, caught in the rafters, his own dayglow Frisbee. The orange freestyle skis. He'd forgotten how much fun he'd had at Burleighwood's ski hill affectionately known as The Spotted Cow.

Livy pulled back some heavy plastic and gravitated toward his grandfather's walnut partner's desk. It was this desk from which his grandfather had waged his rhetorical war against FDR and the New Deal. Livy recalled with a smile that whenever Roosevelt wanted to know the latest Republican fictions, he would ask his advisors what his neighbor Oggie Hitch was saying. His grandfather had harbored resentment of FDR from the thirties and forties, when he had to give ninety percent to the government in taxes after the first $100,000 he earned. In fact, his grandfather started referring to FDR's Springwood as *Crook's Paradise*, and he wasn't referring to the former owner, Charles Crook. Oggie thought FDR was the biggest crook of them all.

When a glint of brass called to him, Livy pulled aside various obstructions. He removed a pile of moth-eaten horse blankets, sneezing from the dust, to reveal an unusual small brass-framed child's bed. Blocking his path to the bed was a vintage red horse-drawn sleigh. The open sleigh was weighed down with boxes. Livy rearranged the boxes and then dragged the bed out into the sunlight. There was a little wired tag wrapped tightly around a bedpost. He could see the name Eleanor Roosevelt elegantly printed on the tag, with Oak Terrace scrawled underneath it. Livy smiled. He had found ER's bed! Hollis had told him the backstory.

A few hours later, Livy returned to the stable to dust off the bed. He had already made the call to the Friends of Eleanor. Frau Flintlock was anticipated at any moment. He looked up, and there, instead, was Jessie.

"So did we find a good place for Valentine's mileage markers?"

"Check it out. What do you think?" Livy said, pointing up to the shelf.

"Looks nice and safe, but how long is that going to last? You think someone with Valentine's sensitivity is going to buy this place and discover these shards of history and recognize their value?"

Livy looked up at her. Her honesty penetrated.

"How old are those again?" she asked.

"Over four hundred years old, laid down back to the early 1600s, when the Post Road was little more than a winding, narrow dirt trail."

Jessie looked around at the accumulation of centuries. "Wow, this place should be exported to the Smithsonian. What else you got in here?"

"I found Eleanor's long-lost childhood bed."

"How do you know it's *the* bed?"

"There's a tag on it on its bedpost."

"What's it say?"

"Eleanor Roosevelt's bed, and I've even alerted Jillian Flintlock."

"Jillian must be thrilled."

Instead of Flintlock in a pickup truck, a shiny, black vintage Rolls Royce came tooling around the lawn circle and to a stop. After thirty seconds of suspense, a very old woman emerged, aided by a driver. A few days earlier, Mosley had received a note from Valentine's oldest living friend announcing that she was coming for her annual tea. Mosley was still processing Valentine's death and had forgotten a most critical appointment with the *queen*, Mrs. Van Rensselaer herself. The tradition dated back to when Livy's grandmother was alive and had continued ever since. Valentine would also get periodic notifications from Mrs. Van Rensselaer. He was gone much of the time photographing, but he always tried to make it back for their traditional yearly tea. The old gal was turning ninety-five that year and would also have to be reminded that Valentine's mother had passed. Livy had not seen Mrs. Van Rensselaer in decades and made a short dash across the lawn to greet her.

"Mrs. Van Rensselaer. It's very nice to see you again. I'm Livingston. Margaret's grandson."

"It's so nice to see you, dear, all grown up. Margaret must be proud."

"You're looking very well, Mrs. Van Rensselaer. To what do we owe this pleasure?"

Withers, her driver, quickly read the awkwardness of the moment. "Mrs. Van Rensselaer is here for her annual tea. The date was confirmed with Mosley."

"Mosley went on vacation and forgot to mention your visit. Not to worry." Livy helped Withers ease the elderly woman into a chair with a view of the river. Amelie Van Rensselaer sat ramrod straight as always, her hair freshly blued for the occasion, although she soon forgot about tea, which relieved everyone.

Mrs. Van Rensselaer launched into a medley of stories spanning the generations. Her narrative spell was interrupted by the sudden arrival of the FOEs. Livy looked up at a woman marching officiously across the lawn.

Flintlock approached the gathering. "I'm here to see Livy Hitch."

Livy looked up at the fearless leader of the FOEs. "I'm your man."

"I received your telephone message," she said briskly.

At that moment, Flintlock realized that their benefactor Amelie Van Rensselaer was sitting with Jessie. Mrs. Van Rensselaer had provided Emerson Winks the money to buy the mall out of receivership and was funding the offer on Burleighwood. Early on, she also bought Winks a yellow seaplane realizing he could monitor the greedy developers and the mess they were making much better from above. Traveling by land didn't reveal the full reality of the onslaught.

"Amelie, how nice to see you!"

"Oh, Jillian. When will Emerson be joining us?"

"He won't be. As I'm sure you know, he's very busy."

Withers whispered into Livy's ear, "Don't forget the big shebang tomorrow."

"What shebang?" Livy asked, rising from his chair.

"The demolition of the mall is Saturday."

"I don't want to miss that. If you'll excuse me. I'll just be a moment." Livy said, then led Flintlock across the lawn to the stable. "The bed is just over here. The tag is attached to the bedpost," Livy said, sensing her impatience. Off to the side of the stable stood the small brass bed.

Jillian approached the bed. "Well, I don't know about the tag, but I know that this is the bed."

Within minutes, the FOEs had already backed up the truck. They loaded the bed into the back of their truck to replace the fake bed that Flintlock had long allowed to pass for the original.

Jessie stood up when Livy returned. "How did it go?"

"Smoothly. Eleanor Roosevelt's bed will soon be back where it belongs."

Mrs. Van Rensselaer hadn't missed a beat, "I do believe Flintlock has a thing for Eleanor."

CHAPTER 12

As Bob Dylan had forecast, the old order was rapidly fading. He neglected to mention that it was also the end of anything civilized.

—Valentine Hitch, *Crook's Paradise*

Emerson Winks's office at Eleanor's childhood home was in the former room of the governess. It was spartan: only two chairs, a desk, and one photograph on the wall, the iconic one of Mrs. Roosevelt carrying her own bags and running across the tarmac in San Francisco to catch her plane, Winks had just gotten off the phone with Fifi the finder.

Fifi had expressed concern that Livy would never agree to sell Burleighwood without a guarantee that the main house would be preserved. Fifi was sick of lawyers referring business, then cutting into her fees. Winks considered her somewhere between a good and bad witch. She had asked him to sit down with Livy, hear him out, then try to talk sense into him.

Winks was mulling this over at his desk. From everything Flintlock had configured, it seemed to him that Livy was a full-on West-coast-whatever-dude surfer. Winks didn't factor in Livy's east coast edge. Getting that Estonian religious sect out of Eleanor's house had been easy because their kids couldn't face spending any more summers in a dreary old house on the Hudson. But Livy was an unknown quantity. Not even the Burleighwood gang he inherited from Valentine could figure him out. No one could doubt his undying devotion to Valentine, but Burleighwood?

Beyond his oak office door, Winks could hear heavy footfalls approaching on the stairs, then huffing and puffing outside the half-open door. Then Livy stood in the doorway, all six-feet-four of him. Winks stood up. "My you're tall. Hello, I'm Emerson Winks."

Livy looked down at Winks and gave his hand a firm shake. "Livy Hitch. My uncle spoke often of you. It's nice to finally put a face with the name."

"Well, please have a seat. I recognize you, of course," Winks said, confusing Livy with *the* Jeff Bridges. "So, you're that actor?"

"Not *that* actor. I act with my voice, it's called voiceovers. I voice-activate the country to eat sugar," Livy chuckled.

"Okay, I get it, you're the sugar frosted flakes guy."

"Close enough."

"Fifi mentioned that you're going back to California, and Burleighwood might be for sale. Boy, that certainly would be good for the community. When FDR died, the Grubb family stepped into the vacuum. Route 9 has been held hostage ever since."

"The *what-were-they-thinking* wasteland that is now Route 9 is a huge concern, but I have other concerns more pressing, closer to home, such as the fate of my family's home. I've heard that the cost of converting

Burleighwood to a guest center would be prohibitive, and that you might be forced to tear it down and start from scratch."

"Well, all things considered, we may not be able to afford to save it. All these mansions are unsustainable. Burleighwood is a money pit, a firetrap. Tourists want convenience. We need wheelchair access, and people wouldn't be stopping here for the historic tour. They come to use the facilities. I know demolishing that house would be a bear for everyone, and especially traumatic for you, but it certainly beats what's happening to Crumwold Hall."

"Sounds like a Hobbesian choice?"

"Oh, yes, that's right, you went to Princeton. Well, I'm sure we both agree that we don't want to replicate the disaster that's happening at the Hall."

"What the hell is happening over there?"

"You know, from my plane, I can see everything, and believe me, these are not good people. They know I'm on to them; it's essentially a no-fly zone."

"Valentine had the same problem with these people."

"I gather that."

"But how is it that such a hallowed Hall has always attracted such a strange batch of the worst kind of people? It was all downhill after the Jesuits."

"That's interesting, you never hear much about the Catholic period."

"Yes, that was after the war, when it became a retreat for Jesuit priests. They treated the place with the utmost respect and could pass muster with Colonel Rogers. They permitted us to play baseball on the lawns just like in the old days when the Colonel's lands were open to everyone in the community to roam and enjoy. Then we had three waves of so-called religious groups that walled themselves in and were more interested in tax evasion than eternal salvation. Now Crumwold has hit a new low, the Grubbs. It's a disaster what's going on over there."

Winks was surprised to find Livy so with-it.

"To be honest, the Grubbs scare me. I've had a glimpse of what's back there. Colonel gifted future generations with thousands of trees, and now all of a sudden, they're gone. I was just over there on my mountain bike. The forest looked like it had been hit by a Vietnam blitz. What was left of the trees looked like dead bodies everywhere. And then, I looked up and some guy had me in his cross hairs. I acknowledged him, and he waved me off with the rifle. Now I know what Valentine must have felt."

Winks sat back contemplating this surge of dark content.

"You know the Grubbs have also attempted to put in a bid a lot higher than yours, and believe me, they'll keep upping it. But you're safe, they aren't even in the discussion."

"Most people in your position would consider themselves lucky to find a buyer who cares about preserving the land like we do."

"Well, obviously, you want the land, but I care about the house more than I thought I would. Indeed, perhaps Burleighwood has not outlived its usefulness. Maybe this is not the end of the story."

Winks didn't like the direction the conversation was suddenly going. "It's certainly a wonderful house. Well, my long-term strategic plan was to join the lands of the big three estates of Crum Elbow, but put yourself in our shoes. How many tourists would actually be interested in Hitch family history? To be honest, I'm just not feeling it."

"Feeling what?"

"The busloads."

"Aren't there preservation grants? The house is a trove of history."

"Whose history?"

"Excuse me?"

"Which history?"

"American History. You know the Founding Fathers, the pursuit of happiness, the rule of law."

"Livy, with all due respect, it's *your* history. Many new Americans don't feel like they share the same history. They can't relate to houses with long driveways. If Eleanor hadn't lived here, do you think this house would still be standing?"

"Yes, I guess Eleanor is a crossover," Livy said.

"Everybody is fascinated by her. She's even more popular than God these days, you know, FDR. Our local deity. When I saw the condition of her childhood place and found out it was for sale, I knew what had to be done. I feel the same way now about Burleighwood."

"This has given me a lot to think about," Livy said.

"Given your financial situation, I don't know how you would manage to maintain Burleighwood."

"What do you know about my financial situation?"

"Well, if you had been that famous actor, you wouldn't need to sell the place."

They both stood up to shake hands. "Thank you for your frankness, Mr. Winks."

"Well, these are tough decisions. I'm trying to make it easier for you."

"Before I depart, I feel I would be remiss not to see Eleanor's long-lost bed in situ."

"Oh, that's right, Livy, you found it. That was Jillian's project."

"So where exactly is the room?"

"Eleanor's room was on the third floor, which was actually the maid's floor and closed to the public. Jillian decided to park the childhood bed in her aunt's much more luxurious bedroom on the second floor. There's a lot of revising always going on."

"Was her childhood that bad?"

"Well, let's just say she had to run to the stables to escape her ugly duckling label. We really play up that part of her childhood because the tourists love it. Flintlock wants to go straight to the first lady of the world and establish Eleanor as the greatest Roosevelt. She wants nothing to do with the ugly duckling on the third floor."

"Well, I'm glad you saved this old place. I've been coming here all my life with Valentine, and every year the house fell more and more into disrepair. I can't believe all the money that's being spent here."

"You can thank Jillian Flintlock. She and the FOEs raised the money overnight."

"Well, I've enjoyed our discussion."

"I've enjoyed meeting you as well, Livy. You certainly know the history of this place."

"For Valentine, everything was a story he loved to tell. I was lucky to have been on the receiving end for so long."

"We're more aligned than you think."

Livy found himself intrigued by the fact that Eleanor had been relegated to the third-floor maids' quarters. The first stop was Aunt Edith's room at the top of the stairs. Her aunt was reputed to have been the inspiration for Lily Bart in Edith Wharton's *House of Mirth*. The large square room had two fireplaces, an eighteen-foot-high ceiling and enormous thirteen-foot windows capturing the stunning views of the Catskills. Her aunt's late-eighteenth-century four-poster bed was the centerpiece. Eleanor's childhood brass bed had been placed in an alcove with an arched opening. The childhood bed appeared always to have been in the room, though it had replaced her aunt's harp on the classical Turkish carpet.

Livy then ascended the ponderous, dark-wooded stairs to take a look at Eleanor's original room. If walls could talk, these stairs were tellin' it. The maids quarters on the third floor were unusually small. Even the molding tapered off. Eleanor's was a tiny room at the end of the hallway. Livy stood at the door for a moment, feeling the sadness in the room.

He made his way back down the stairs and exited the impressive door of the mansion house, back into the fragrance of the river valley. He stood outside in a river dream, fondly recalling his walks to the springs with Valentine. His uncle was certain that the water had healing qualities and feared some entrepreneur would discover the springs and start bottling the water. The very thought of the spring water made him feel closer to Valentine. He circled around the house and found the trail. He was amazed how fast nature grew back. Valentine's trail to the springs had disappeared with him. Livy trampled the bramble and descended several small rock ledges. He missed Valentine's narrative. Valentine would periodically stop, listen, and comment on the intelligence of nature. When Livy arrived at Valentine's secret spot, he heard the sound of a person approaching and looked up. "Well, I'll be darned. If it isn't Saint Benedict, himself."

"And I'll be darned if it isn't Valentine's favorite nephew. I thought I saw someone coming down here. I was expecting Valentine, but it's great to see you, Livy."

"I'm sorry to have to be the one to tell you, Beano, but Valentine passed away. I know you two were close."

Beano removed his hat and put it over his heart for a moment. He looked down at Valentine's bubbling diamond water, as if hoping to feel Valentine smiling on him. "What happened?"

"His heart gave out on a train. It was quick. It's hard to imagine we're never going to see him again."

Beano seemed frustrated. "I don't know why, but I can't locate his spirit the way I usually can."

"You can actually see them, huh?"

"No, I hear them."

"What's Valentine saying?"

"I can feel and hear him, but he's not saying anything."

"You communicate with the dead?"

"I hear them. I don't know if they hear me, but I hear them."

"When did you first realize you can do this?"

"My grandmother discovered it. She had the same gift. She called it our 'ladder to Heaven.' She would always find me talking to my grandpa, and he was twenty-years-dead. You wouldn't believe all the invisible people I talk to, especially along the Hudson. But Valentine hasn't checked in yet." He paused, shaking his head. "This only happened to me once, and it turned out the person wasn't dead."

Walking back to the parking lot, Livy noticed Valentine's Pierce-Arrow was attracting attention. Some visitors wondered if it was Eleanor's car. The encounter with Beano left him feeling unsettled. It would have been a séance, but Valentine was a no show.

CHAPTER 13

Instead of eating up the landscape, it's time to reverse course and begin undeveloping, redeveloping, and restoring.

—Valentine Hitch, *Crook's Paradise*

Livy woke the next morning with a different outlook. He had stayed up late reading and underlining words in the manuscript of Valentine's swan song. He recognized that his uncle was speaking to him. He was alive in his head. By the time Livy finished the draft, Valentine had gotten to him. Valentine's voice was everywhere in his mind. He impressed upon his nephew that Burleighwood was relevant in a million ways. His uncle thought the only way to reclaim the Hudson Valley from the mall beast was with divinely-chosen bulldozing. It was his modest Swiftian proposal, an armchair fantasy that reflected sheer idealism. He never thought we'd ever see such a thing. But his link with Winks was turning out to be a key factor. Livy was even starting to appreciate Winks's ballsy approach. Valentine never could talk sense into the town leaders. Then Winks showed up and gave everyone hope. He was doing what Valentine never thought possible. Everyone had heard of urban renewal. Winks had become the face of suburban removal, or to use Valentine's phrase, "bulldozer conservation." Winks had the backing and the necessary balls to actually do it. Winks was clever. He had visited all the wealthy widows and landowners in the Hudson Valley to plead his case for reclaiming the land along the river at Crum Elbow. They remembered how that stretch of land used to look and were upset with what had happened to the historic bend in the river. Winks got them to open their checkbooks. They were an easy sell; they had the money and the memory. The only problem was that the dude had enemies. He was seen as a New Age Robin Hood. He'd been provoking some really rich developers for a while, and they now had him in the crosshairs. Of course, the town board wasn't very happy about turning taxable land into parkland. They didn't like losing a revenue stream. But, now that Winks owned the shopping center next door to Burleighwood, he could do anything he wanted with it.

Livy had been sitting on the front steps waiting for Jessie to join him but lost his patience and went to seek her out. He headed down the front steps of the mansion, crossed the lawn circle, and walked the meandering dirt carriage road out past Tad's barn. Farther down the road, he spotted Jessie standing in the sun, at the edge of her fields talking with one of her farm hands.

Livy soaked up Jessie's radiance for a moment before he called out to her. "Aren't you going to come to the demolition derby and watch Winks whack the mall?"

"It's not my fight anymore," Jessie said.

"What do you mean? He's making Valentine's dream come to life."

"Yes, but it won't bring Valentine back to life, and that makes me sad. Only *you* can bring him back."

Livy didn't have any clue what to say to that one. There was not enough dopamine in his brain to process it. "Me?"

Jessie surveyed her garden of "eatins."

"Let me go freshen up, and I'll join you."

The citizens of Crum Elbow had shown up en masse, polarizing between pro-beautification and pro-growth. There weren't many middle-grounders or much of a loyal opposition. The crowd had already begun staking out its territory. Yellow police tape defined a fifty-foot perimeter around a big beast of a bulldozer, its mighty blade aimed like a tank at the mall, built in 1958. The Cat D-11 had been contributed to the cause by a donor who preferred to remain nameless. This beast could make mincemeat of the mall.

Livy took Jessie's hand and led the way through the crowd to find a quieter spot. "If it weren't for Winks, I would have thought Valentine's ideas were pure fantasy."

"Valentine was sort of a past-futurist. He only cared about the past if it could bring about a better future," said Jessie. "A man like Valentine is one in a billion. Winks is quite the operator, but the vision started with Valentine."

Smiling in his crisp blue suit, Emerson Winks surprised everyone by ducking under the police tape and climbing up the tracks of the bulldozer. Once he found a good place to hold on, he was able to steady himself above the crowd. He lightly tapped the microphone and waited for the people of Crum Elbow to settle themselves.

Livy heard a rumble of boos all around. "With all the hot buttons he's pushing, I imagine he's now in the Grubbs' crosshairs."

"Yeah, and then with a hair-trigger," Jessie agreed.

Taking firm hold, Winks launched into his speech. "My friends, Crum Elbow is dying. We've given away the farm to outsiders with deep pockets and no conscience. The landowner cashes out, and we're stuck with ugly. The franchise vacuums up local revenue and makes a direct deposit into the deep pockets of far-away shareholders."

Heads were nodding in agreement. Winks surfed the swell with surging confidence. "And have any of you benefited?"

"No!" and "Hell no!" rang out from the crowd.

"You tell 'em, Winks!" Livy called out.

"I didn't expect such eloquence," Jessie said.

"My friends, Crum Elbow once thrived. It was a small town that had a knack for drawing international attention. Business was local. Destiny was ours to shape. Now we've surrendered power to people who don't even live here. Look at what happened to Ralph Peterson. We all used to shop at Peterson's Hardware Store. Ralph, how many generations did your family own the store?"

"Four!" Peterson called out. "My great-grandfather founded it."

"And what happened, Ralph?" Winks asked.

"The big boxes moved into town, and look. We're out of business."

"That's right, folks. The whole town's outta business. Your town has changed beyond recognition. I don't see people on the sidewalks anymore. All I see are cars. Main Street used to be for local folks. Now it's a highway. There are cars everywhere. The town feels like one continuous parking lot. Our town's leadership would rather make the cars happy than making nature happy. Have the good citizens of Crum Elbow noticed that we have lost our town to pure sprawl?"

Winks paused for full effect. Applause and a few boos rippled through the crowd. "I'm angry at what our mayor and town leaders have allowed to happen to our heritage. Enough is enough! If you can't beat 'em, buy it back and bulldoze."

Jessie turned away from the main event and noticed a Ford Crown Victoria with darkened windows. She nudged Livy. "Don't look now but there's something creepy about that car parked way off by itself."

"Yeah, I already noticed the dark windows."

Jessie looked over at Livy, "Let's get away from these people."

"Ok, follow me, we're going to move towards the front," Livy said as they merged into the crowd.

All attention turned to Valentine's hero, Aldo the bulldozer operator. He climbed into the cab, turned the key on, released the emergency brake, and tilted the joystick slightly to the right to adjust the blade.

Winks clenched his fist and shook it. Then he grabbed the mic and cried out, "Let the mall fall. Let the mall fall down."

*   *   *

News of the demolition of the mall that had desecrated the historic bend in the river since the fifties exploded in the media. Winks, with his mall-eating grin, appeared on the cover of *Time Magazine*. He testified before a Senate subcommittee on suburban sprawl. He was practically sainted by the green movement. He was on the many Sunday morning talk shows spreading the message of Bulldozer Conservation. Every town in America had some remnant of outside dark money that it wanted to tear down. Winks became the voice of everyday people who wondered why the country was intent on rebuilding nations overseas, instead of rebuilding dying towns and cities back at home. Winks became small-town America's hero. All he needed was a guitar.

Emerson Winks had always assumed that the restoration of the Eleanor Roosevelt historic site would be the culmination of his life's work. He had never expected to leave or retire. He didn't know how it happened, but he had ended up fighting for the town. Saving Crum Elbow had seemed like a logical step after restoring Eleanor's house. Where the town fathers saw strip malls and asphalt parking lots, Winks envisioned *Crum Elbow meets Shangri-La*. Their visions couldn't have been further apart.

Winks realized that to make changes in Crum Elbow, he needed power. He decided to run for mayor in November. Over the next couple of weeks villagers started seeing red, white, and blue *THINK WINKS* signs posted on front lawns.

One evening, on her way home from yoga, Jessie passed Jillian Flintlock and a brigade of FOEs bearing armfuls of *THINK WINKS* campaign signs.

It looked surreal to see, the women scattering throughout the neighborhood at dusk stapling the *THINK WINKS* signs to the telephone poles.

As she approached Burleighwood, Jessie could see the lights on in Tad's shop and Hollis's jeep parked outside. The day had been warm, but the night was cold. The incessant sound of cicadas thrummed everywhere. Jessie couldn't escape it. The sound of Tad banging against metal actually sounded like music to her ears. Inside, she found Livy and Hollis standing around Livy's car. Tad's muffled voice came from beneath the car. It had been two weeks since the car had sunk and flooded, and Tad still couldn't get it running properly.

"I'm doing my best," Tad shouted from beneath the Volvo.

"You've come at an opportune time, Jessie," Hollis said.

"We're discussing how we all feel about Winks's candidacy for Mayor," said Livy.

"He's a bum," Tad shouted.

"Why don't you tell us the way you really feel, Tad," Hollis said, winking at Livy and Jessie.

"He's not getting my vote," Tad said gruffly.

Hollis raised his eyebrows, "What are you talking about, Tad? You're not even registered to vote."

Tad was one of the uncounted. He had never voted in a presidential election, or any election for that matter. He had never served on a jury. He ran a cash business. He was off the grid, or so he thought.

Jessie warned Tad, "If you don't vote, you have no right to complain."

"Yes, well, I may register just so I can vote against Winks."

Hollis turned to Jessie and Livy. "Somehow I doubt that Tad represents the tipping point in the election."

"Look, Tad," Jessie said. "Granted he's a kook. I don't like him either, but he might be exactly what Crum Elbow needs."

"At the risk of pissing off Tad, I agree with Jessie. Winks certainly has his issues, but he's a doer," Hollis said.

Tad stopped banging and slid out from underneath the car. Livy reached out and offered him a hand up. "I'm good," Tad said. He rolled off the dolly, grabbed his trusty rope hanging from a rafter, pulled himself up onto a stool, and reattached his other leg. "I think everyone knows Winks wants Burleighwood. The word in my shop is that he's in discussion with Livy."

"I haven't agreed to anything. At least he's not a criminal. You don't trust me?"

"You just don't have as much to lose," Jessie responded.

"East Coasters don't appreciate the value of flow. You think of it as a character defect."

"I'm sorry, Livy, but at this point, I'm more interested in bucking bad flow," Jessie said.

Tad wiped his big, rough, greasy hands on a shop rag. "I'm with you, Jessie. Everyone knows my friend Aldo; he freelances as Winks's bulldozer operator. Winks told Aldo that after he bulldozed the mall, Mildew Manor was next."

"I don't even know what the hell you're talking about, Tad," Livy said.

"Mildew Manor is Winks's new name for Burleighwood."

"I'm not feeling any empathy happening here, Livy," Jessie said, starting to agree with Tad.

"What's up with that? You don't give a shit about us," Tad said.

"Full stop requested. I'm not the enemy. I just feel overwhelmed."

Tad looked at Jessica. Jessie looked at Tad. For once they were on the same side.

*   *   *

The next morning, Jessie was coming out of the post office when she ran into Livy. "How about tea at the diner?" she said.

"Ah, perfect, the New Deal Diner, there's hope."

They crossed the street and Livy opened the door to the diner. Jessie led the way to the counter. Jessie asked the waitress about their tea selection, to which the waitress replied, "Lipton, Lipton, and Lipton."

"Perfect, make it two cups of Lipton," Jessie said, turning to smile at Livy.

Cosmo Papas, with a happy-hour grin, emerged from the kitchen. He wore a short-sleeve shirt adorned with a half-dozen THINK WINKS buttons. Cosmo wiped his hands on a kitchen towel. He dug into his pockets, fished out a handful of buttons, and began handing them out to everyone at the counter. He commented to Jessie, "There's something missing from your outfit, pretty lady."

Jessie cheerfully fixed the button to her shirt. Livy stood up and shook Cosmo's hand.

"Oh, Livy. I've missed you. It's been sad without Valentine."

"I know, we all go so far back."

"Valentine was always my favorite person. He had something kind to say about everyone," Cosmo said, looking up at the person sitting next to Jessie. "Well, almost everyone."

Ed Williams, the town planning board's protector of dark money, sat silently and stared at his eggs sunny-side-up. Cosmo tried to hand Ed a *THINK WINKS* button but was turned away. It seemed Ed would have preferred to put Winks in a burlap bag with rocks and dump him into the Hudson. Under Ed's leadership and Grubb family funding, the town planning board had been properly shackled and repurposed.

After finishing her tea, Jessie leaned across Livy. "Good morning, Mr. Williams."

Ed growled back, "Good morning."

She looked at Livy. "Most people think the church group still lives at Crumwold Hall. What do you think, Ed? Aren't you on the planning board?"

"I'm the chairman."

"Well, can you enlighten us, Mr. Chair?" Jessie asked.

Ed continued to obfuscate. Livy spoke up, "FDR always boiled the world's problems down to local ones. Dealing with a neighbor. He used the example of lending your neighbor a garden hose if their house were on fire. If FDR were alive today, and Crumwold Hall were on fire, and he ran next door to lend them a hose, he wouldn't get past the razor wire, or two feet onto their property before the flood lights came on, they'd release the dogs on him and shoot him dead in his tracks," Livy said.

"I thought he had polio," cited Ed.

"That wouldn't have stopped him. That was a time of decency," Livy said.

"What do you think, Ed? What's the deal over there?" Jessie asked.

"Hey, at least these guys pay taxes," Ed said. There was a long silence. He paid his bill and grunted in lieu of saying goodbye.

Cosmo rolled his eyes in disgust. "Yeah, those crooks paying taxes? I doubt it."

Jessie turned to Livy, "Now you've seen first-hand what Valentine was up against. I wonder if any of us will want to be living here in six months. What you think, Livy? It's probably time to bail," she said, squeezing more honey into her tea.

CHAPTER 14

As Yogi Berra said, "The future just ain't what it used to be."
The millennials are inheriting a boat without a paddle.

—Valentine Hitch, *Crook's Paradise*

It proved too much for Ed Williams when Winks announced his candidacy for mayor. He met privately with J. Homer Grubb, 3.0, who looked as if he rarely missed a meal. 3.0 was used to opposition but represented a more enlightened kind of crookery. His father, Homer Junior, was old school. He'd built his company on arson, blackmail, and bribery. He never even heard of e-mail. But times had changed. 3.0 was college educated. He was a cyber whizz and had discovered that he could better control reality along the Hudson with a computer. 3.0 was completely aloof from his father's generation. He had never even been to the main office. He insisted on total autonomy. When the Grubbs invaded Crumwold Hall, the isolation of the tower enchanted him. He was part lone wolf and part night owl.

Ed Williams was the first to arrive at the parking lot of Poet's Walk. He was listening to the Yankees beat the Phillies. When 3.0 pulled up alongside him, they looked at each other through several layers of glass. When they rolled their windows down, Williams could hear that Grubb 3.0 was also listening to the Yankees. "Three and two. Full count and here comes the pitch, bye, bye birdie. It's a long fly ball to center field. It's outta here. Gone. Kiss it goodbye."

"Well, what do you know, you show up, and a Yankee hits a home run, Homer. What's going on with the other game? If we don't act fast, Winks is going to enlist that agitator Pete Seeger to sing about Bulldozer Conservation down on the Clearwater," Ed said.

"You don't have to worry about Pete Seeger; he's a hundred years old."

"Thank you for discouraging Valentine from taking any more photographs, but how are we going to stop Winks?"

Emerson Winks had long since become a thorn in the Grubb agenda. 3.0 had been monitoring Winks's e-mails, cell phone, and Google searches for the past two years.

"So what's the deal," Ed sniffed.

"I couldn't find a trace of Winks before the late eighties," he said, showing Ed a picture of a much heavier, grizzled man.

"Who is this with the beard?"

"That's Winks."

"That's him?"

"That's him. This is gold. Turns out his real name is Pruitt McVeigh."

"Sounds like the Oklahoma bomber."

"No relation, but he may get executed some day, too."

"Why, what did he do?"

"He's wanted for arson and manslaughter and a whole host of other eco-crimes."

Mulling over Winks's newly discovered vulnerabilities, Ed said, "I've got an idea."

*   *   *

3.0 had been absorbed inside the Internet for hours. He finally took a break and opened the tower windows for fresh air. He looked out the window at the slow-moving, moonlit river, where ocean tides and mountain water merge, where the suburban meets the pastoral. Suddenly, his nose was arrested by something burning. He saw flames over the tree line. He grabbed the larger fire extinguisher and ran down the stairs. He burst from the back-door entrance of the tower, still on his cell phone.

Watching from the safety of hemlock shadow, Hollis and Tad waited until the coast was clear. "The diversion worked," Tad said, very pleased with himself. When Tad had gone to Tanner and his skateboard followers with a plan to help fulfill Valentine's last photograph, there was not a moment's hesitation. There was nothing these guys wouldn't do for Mr. Hitch.

"Let's go, Hollis. No time to waste. You run up the stairs, take your photos, and get out. Two minutes max."

"What's plan B?"

"One-minute max. If he comes back, I'll beep you, Hollis. You get your ass out the window to the balcony, and I'll have the ladder set up."

"I don't think I can do this, Tad. I'm freaking."

Tad looked Hollis straight in the eye. "Fuck it, give me that camera. I'll take the damn picture. Go back and hide in the bushes, Hollis."

Hollis hesitated, took his camera out of its case, and was about to hand it to Tad, then stopped and weighed the camera in his hand like a revolver. "No, I need to take this picture."

"Well, then get your ass in there."

"You're the only guy I trust, Tad," Hollis said and took off for the door. He followed the featherbone tiles through the great hall. Hollis figured he must have climbed over thirty stairs to the half-open door of the tower room. From Valentine's stories, he had expected to step into the vast digital network of glistening military-grade technology. But all he saw was a futon on the floor and a brightly lit-up laptop. The first thing he did was look out the window to check on the bonfire burning on the riverbanks, at the site of the old swimming pavilion. Valentine's *rough riders* had heaved a dilapidated picnic table into the bonfire, then made their getaway before 3.0 arrived for a fireside chat.

There was nothing worth documenting. Nonetheless, Hollis photographed the room anyway. He took one last look out the tower window in the direction of the fire and spotted Grubb 3.0 coming back across the lawn. "Oh shit," he muttered and backtracked down the steps and along the marbled corridor. As he approached the entrance hall and heard the front door opening, he ducked into a tiny vestibule. He assessed the cerebral dude with Gucci loafers and gold chains around his neck. No visible tattoos. Seconds later, after 3.0 had gone upstairs, Hollis was able to sneak out.

Back in the darkroom, Hollis had pulled the prints from a chemical bath. Then he pulled up a chair at the worktable, half of which was covered by chapters of Valentine's manuscript.

"Not what Valentine expected," Hollis said. "The room was practically empty. There was nothing there but a laptop. What happened to all the high-tech shit? Was this all for nothing?"

"The world is run from a laptop today. I know that Valentine was onto something. And you did find something," Tad said.

"What did I find?" asked Hollis.

"You found your balls!"

*   *   *

The next morning, Grubb 3.0 stared out from a tower window for the interlopers. He tucked his laptop into his briefcase and made his way down the steps. For the first time, he spied the quote over the fireplace, the Latin phrase: *Post Tenebras Lux*, "After the darkness, light." He could see that Colonel Rogers was a believer. Seems they all were back then. He ducked out the front door and got into his car and headed out of the driveway.

Full of purpose, Emerson Winks pulled up in front of his campaign headquarters, located in the showroom of the former Buick dealership, across from the fieldstone Post Office. There were *THINK WINKS* signs plastered all over the plate-glass windows. Winks got out of his car to face an army of reporters and TV cameramen. He had barely reached the curb before the barrage of questions began.

"Why do you hate free enterprise?"

"Are you a communist?"

"Do you believe in private property?"

"Do you like trees better than people?"

"What is your obsession with Eleanor Roosevelt?"

Winks did not deign to answer the questions. But, as he stood there, his back to traffic, a Ford Crown Victoria slowly cruised past like a hungry tiger shark. Then someone lowered the darkened car window and called, "Hey, Pruitt, Mr. McVeigh. So, it's McVeigh for Mayor. It's got a ring to it."

Winks turned around and froze. His life as he knew it was over and, boy, did he know it. He had been prepared for the day when he might have to walk out on his life in a moment's notice. He had even kept a bag packed.

*   *   *

Livy stood at the counter of the local Sunoco on the main drag. As he was waiting for credit card approval, Carla Jensen of WTBY-TV interrupted the regular programing to report from the banks of the Hudson at Crum Elbow.

"At three o'clock this afternoon, Emerson Winks, the director of the Eleanor Roosevelt National Historic Site and mayoral candidate, apparently lost control of his plane and is presumed dead. I'm here with Emmett Stone, a doctoral student in hydrology from UC Berkeley, who saw the plane just before it crashed. Emmett, please tell us what you saw?"

Livy asked the attendant, "Can you turn up the volume on the TV? I know that guy."

The television camera zoomed in on Emmett Stone. He was dressed in khaki shorts that extended past his knees, a Phish T-shirt, and a baseball cap with a fish logo.

"I was taking water samples when a low-flying seaplane disappeared into the clouds. I heard the crash and soon after the sirens. Everything seems to find its way into the Hudson river these days."

"Well, thank you for coming forth, Mr. Stone. Emerson Winks, forty-nine, was running for mayor on his Bulldozer Conservation platform. His death is a big shock for the community here in Dutchess County. Emerson Winks's body has yet to be recovered. No further details have been released. Anyone with information is asked to contact the New York State Police hotline."

Within a few hours, emails were circulating with pictures of Winks's seaplane being lifted out by a barge crane. That afternoon, the tabloids and network TV crews descended on Crum Elbow like locusts to cover the story. The media trucks choked Route 9. The town square was crowded with curious onlookers, and the police were out in force trying to maintain order. Winks's supporters made a shrine out of the front steps of his campaign headquarters. Hundreds of bouquets of flowers and candles appeared. By midday, Winks had almost been sainted—until, from the courthouse steps, CNN Reporter Barry Reasoner broke the national news story of an entirely different Emerson Winks. "We've just learned new information about Emerson Winks's true identity. Believe it or not, this is what Emerson Winks looked like in the late eighties," Reasoner said, cutting to a mug-shot of a man who looked like Abbie Hoffman. Thanks to fasting, a haircut and shave, not to mention plastic surgery, there was no resemblance to the man who had championed Eleanor Roosevelt.

"It turns out that Crum Elbow's mayoral candidate Emerson Winks's real name is Pruitt McVeigh, and he is wanted by the FBI for eco-terror and manslaughter. It comes as a shock to us all and certainly changes the story of the man who briefly stood on the same pedestal as FDR in Crum Elbow. The Sheriff's office reminds us that until the body is found, the case remains open."

*   *   *

Jillian Flintlock heard the news about Winks's death on her car radio and immediately returned to her office to sit by the phone. Winks was still her hero. Impatiently, she looked at the clock, waiting for the guards to make their final pass through the historic house before leaving for the evening.

Ten minutes later, Flintlock stood at the window and watched the taillights of the psychic park ranger Beano's late-model station wagon disappear down the driveway.

Moments later, the phone rang at her desk, three single-ring-calls punctuated by silences. Then it stopped. She stepped across the hallway and stood at the entrance of the bedroom that she had so fastidiously recreated from photographs. All that separated her was the red velvet rope barrier. Jillian raised her leg and lifted her knee as high as she could to straddle the rope, then she lowered her leg on the other side. Her other leg followed. The moonlight over the Hudson illuminated a corner of the bed. Jillian sat on the bed and leaned back against a pillow and curled up like a child on top of the carefully curated bed and escaped into a dream world.

The following day, Jillian Flintlock got busy removing the *THINK WINKS* posters that were still hanging in the showroom window. Livy had left the post office and gotten back into the Pierce-Arrow parked across the street from the campaign headquarters, when he noticed movement behind a huge poster with the picture of Winks with his toothy grin. Suddenly, the poster came down—revealing Jillian Flintlock. What still puzzled him was the enigma Flintlock seemed intent upon concealing.

"Just what did she know, and when did she know it?"

CHAPTER 15

You rarely see the new breed of crooks. All you see is the result: unemployed and unemployable fifty-year-olds looking for a ride.

—Valentine Hitch, *Crook's Paradise*

Now that the only respectable potential buyer of Burleighwood was dead, the future looked grim to Livy. Winks's plane going down had created an ominous vacuum. Strange magnetics attracted and repelled him. He was starting to miss his surfboard.

That evening, Livy met with each person separately to discuss the future of Burleighwood, at least his lawyer's version; the dining room table was covered with legal documents and stacks of paperwork. This is when Tad and Hollis fully grasped the terms of Valentine's bequest of lifetime tenancy. They were in limbo with Livy. It turned out Valentine had made Livy the final arbiter. Livy had expected Jessie as well. He was concerned that Jessie hadn't shown up. He looked at his watch thinking, "For goodness's sake, Jessie could have at least called."

Hollis, who always seemed to know what was going on, told Livy that Jessie had called the lawyer and came to the full realization that she was screwed. She then announced that she needed a drink and was headed to Elsie's.

"What's Elsie's?"

"It's a karaoke bar in Barrytown, popular with Bard College students."

"I had a meeting scheduled with her. She's gone out drinking?"

"She remembered the meeting and said she'd be back by eight," Hollis explained.

"It's nine o'clock, Hollis. Is this a regular thing?"

"This is the first time I've heard of Elsie's."

"I hope she's alright." Livy said.

"Maybe she's on a date," Hollis speculated.

"That's all I need to hear. Time to find her."

"You're the one driving her to drink," Hollis said.

"Listen, it's not my intention to be the bad guy."

"I know that. You're a good man. Livy, what you're not seeing is that Jessie could be done farming here tomorrow. She was here for Valentine as much as the farm. Now she's in uncharted waters. She wants family. She loves Burleighwood. Valentine was like family to her. Burleighwood has been her compass."

Livy felt like he had just fallen through a door in the floor.

"I don't think you realize what you have here. I'm surprised she didn't bail already."

"Wait, why am I the bad guy all of the sudden?"

"You're not the bad guy, Livy. You're the future. Just not the one she envisioned."

Livy found Elsie's Okie Dokie Karaoke Bar on the ground floor of the old firehouse on the river. The railroad tracks ran between the river and the bar. Elsie's shook every time the high-speed Amtrak Empire

Service train roared past. It was a happening place. Livy parked in front and walked into the dimly lit bar area and looked around. A crush of college students at the bar sang along with a familiar voice. The karaoke was taking place at the far end of the room on a small stage and there sat Jessie singing like Bonnie Raitt. Even the bar potatoes had spun around on their stools facing the warm glow that had appeared in the air.

Livy loved that Jessie could sing. The words flew out of her heart like birds. Even the college boys were dazzled by her sensuality.

When the song ended, the crowd roared approval. She was a star, plain and simple. Livy glared at the cat-caller behind him. He seemed to be about to say something; then he realized he was vastly outnumbered and turned back around. It seemed fruitless anyway. They were college students. Hormones were popping. The next singer tripped over the speaker cord and splashed her drink into a sea of inebriation. Livy was there to offer his hand as Jessie stepped off the stage.

"Ah, the patroon is lending a helping hand. What are you doing here?"

"Me? What the hell are you doing here? We had a meeting scheduled. Where the heck were you?"

"Singing my heart out. Look, evidently there's no future here for me," Jessie said as they walked past the line of eager singers. "You have California and some kind of a future that doesn't include any of us. Aren't you being kind of a dick? I'm just saying."

"Ah, a few drinks and out comes the truth."

"Well, it's a good thing it did. I guess it takes a few drinks to set you straight."

"Maybe I should have a drink to tell you what I'm really feeling," Livy said, standing.

"Great, I'll have another vodka and soda with a touch of cranberry."

By the time Livy returned with the drinks, Jessie had company. "Hey Livy, meet Jared. We were talking about Walt Whitman. Jared is an English major."

Livy handed Jessie the drink and looked down at Jared. "Hey buddy, three's a crowd, maybe it's time to go roll some leaves of grass?"

Jared stood up. "Here's your seat back, old man."

"Older and wiser," Livy said and sat back down. "Sorry to interrupt your little party."

"Look Livy, I don't think there's much to talk about. You do you. Go back to your beach in California. And I'll do me."

"I guess that's my answer."

"What's that?"

"That I need to get you home."

"I was going to call a cab."

"No need. You're coming with me. We'll get your car in the morning."

A gaggle of students stood outside the bar smoking. In a move of delicious self-sabotage, Jessie copped a cigarette from one of the students, parked herself against a tree, and puffed, looking through the branches at the river.

Livy walked over to join her. "Really, a cigarette?"

"Once in a while, I indulge, so let's have our meeting here," she said, stamping out her cigarette. "So, what are your plans, Mr. Legacy?"

"Well, tonight it's getting you home safely."

"I appreciate that. I'm not feeling so good right now," Jessie said, then bent over, seemed ill for a moment, and then recovered. "Cigarettes and booze, bad combo. It's time for bed. My head hurts."

Once in Livy's car, Jessie eased the seat back and conked out on the ride home. For the next twenty-five minutes, Livy snaked his way along County Road 103 through the dark Ferncliff Forest, and then back onto Route 9 south to Burleighwood.

On the way down the gravel driveway, Livy looked at the *For Sale* sign. Winks had been the ideal buyer. Had he sold to Winks, Livy could have lived with himself. The words *For Sale* looked weirdly out of place.

The next day, Jessie was back on her hands and knees. Instead of a day off, she'd slept in an extra hour and got to the fields by 8:00 a.m. As the sun rose in the sky, Jessie looked up from her planting and saw a familiar figure coming her way. She recognized Valentine's rumpled old blue canvas jacket. Jessie rose up from her knees. "Thanks for the ride home. I'm going to need a ride back to get my car."

"Yes, and we're still due for our meeting."

"There's nothing for me to sign, Livy."

"I don't know if you realize it, but I inherited Burleighwood without the money to take care of it for more than a few years."

"Seems like a failure of imagination. Your namesake Philip Livingston erected a giant chain that stretched all the way across the Hudson to keep the British invaders out," she said, crossing her arms.

Livy stopped and listened. "Okay. And?"

"That dude had something. You need to be *that* guy and stretch a chain around Burleighwood."

"Wow, I've never been compared with Philip the Signer."

She took off her gloves and handed them to him. "I'll be back. I have a travel reservation to check on."

"Wait a minute. This is your busy season."

"Yes, and the clock is ticking."

"What about your plants?"

"My pact's been fulfilled. You know, the one with Valentine to bring the farm back. Take a look. It's back. Now you're selling Burleighwood, and I'm moving back out West." She marched off to make her call.

All of the sudden it hit him. Valentine's vision of the future wasn't just about Burleighwood. It was more about putting people together that belonged together. Livy got down on his knees, pulled up a handful of weeds, shook the dirt off their roots, and began filling up a wheelbarrow. By the time Jessie returned, the wheelbarrow was overflowing with dandelions. "Wow, you already filled it."

"It's tough on the legs, but it sure feels good."

"Keep connecting. There's lots of garlic to be planted. And asparagus."

"I think it's time for me to go to New York and figure this out," Livy said.

CHAPTER 16

Everything important once arrived by river. The Hudson had always been the leading character in the story. Now there's a crook in the elbow and carcinogens in the river.

—Valentine Hitch, Crook's Paradise

The full day he spent in the sun and the fresh air of the river breeze had done Livy good. His body was tired but felt surprisingly more awake, curiously fearless of the future.

The following day, Livy had a lunch date with his long-time agent Bud Nathanson. Bud was in New York auditioning voices to become the spokesman of Vampire Bites cereal. Livy had no plans to become a cartoon and had declined to audition, but he had been looking forward to see Bud. A lot had happened since he had first turned up his nose at Vampire Bites.

Livy and Bud met for lunch at the Grove Hotel, just off lower Seventh Avenue South at Sheridan Square in the West Village. The Grove was near the old jazz clubs and where John Barrymore used to live. It was a wonderful area of New York that often doubled for old Europe in film. The streets were paved with eighteenth-century cobblestones and huge Belgian blocks that had made it to New York as ships' ballast during the nineteenth century. The Grove was in an ornate, landmark building. Planted at the entrance of the Ming Dynasty-inspired dining room was a round, marble, smiling Buddha. Livy rubbed the Buddha's belly for good luck and saw Bud waving from across the room. The maître d' escorted him over to the table. Bud stood up to shake Livy's hand, and Livy embraced him.

"It's wonderful to see you, Liv. I'm very sorry about your uncle. I know he played an important role in your life."

"I loved that man. I dearly miss him."

"How are you enjoying being back East?"

"I've come from a place where everyone is just passing through and arrived at a place where people never leave. My family's house has been at Crum Elbow, overlooking the river for three hundred years."

"In Los Angeles, we're proud of being in business since 1970." Bud chuckled, then turned around and signaled to the waiter. He came over, served them coffee, and took their order.

"I've been dealing with three hundred years of accumulation."

"How's that working out?"

"Inheriting Burleighwood has complicated my life. That's why you haven't heard from me. For a while, I had a buyer, but he turned out to be a terrorist."

"Yeah, I read about that. What's the upshot?"

"I'm starting to feel something I haven't felt in a long time," Livy said with a smile.

Bud could feel the change in Livy's barometric levels. He sensed his surrender. Livy didn't seem to be in any hurry to go anywhere. His journey had washed the California coastal desert right out of him. "Wow, Livy, there's something different about you. What's going on? I'm thinking it's good. What's her name?"

"How'd you know?"

"You've got that glow."

"Jessica Chandler."

"And?"

"Jessie is farming the land at Burleighwood. It's a long story, but she's been there for almost two years. She's really done me a lot of good."

"Are you in love?"

Livy nodded.

"Is it mutual?"

"We met about three years ago and stupid me went back to La La Land and never called her back. I hope I'm not too late."

"That's 'cause you were living with *what's her name.*"

"Don't remind me. I feel bad enough. I'm making up for lost time now. Any word from the world's favorite fix?"

"I'm afraid that Coke's new brand manager wants Clint Eastwood's voice. It's still all about star power."

"I guess I'm going to have to reinvent."

"Great attitude."

"What's the story with Vampire Bites? That little fanged fellow with the purple cape?"

"Well, as you know, the audition's Friday."

"Someone die? What happened to the last Count?"

"He didn't scare the kids anymore."

"Well, it's still a vulture culture, but it sounds like the little Count needs an upgrade," Livy said.

"Well, the last time they gave the little Count a makeover, they tried to make him hip. They gave him an electric guitar on the cover of the box."

"Just like Coca-Cola's makeover into New Coke. There doesn't seem to be anything wrong with classic," Livy said.

"I'll give you that. Last we spoke, you had no interest in cartoon roles. I didn't sign you up for the audition."

"Well, can you still get me in? Now, thanks to Clint, I'm down for the count."

"You don't realize, cartoons have gone to another level. They rule."

"Our *culture* has become a giant cartoon," Livy concurred, "But the little count is kind of a wimp, even with the guitar."

"Well, that's the challenge. I've been around your sub-personalities for years. I'm sure you've got all kinds of vampires in there, and don't forget, the residuals might last for the rest of your life. You won't need the Coke account. Sooner or later, we all become typecast. So, that's a yes on the count?" Bud asked.

"It's a yes, a yes to a lot of things."

"Adulthood seems to suit you well."

"When you get the right woman, it sure is easier."

"That's when you'll really need the count residuals."

"Tell me about it."

"You're now the man of the manor."

"Much as I love Burleighwood, if it weren't for Jessie, I'd be back in LA."

After lunch, Bud looked at his watch and signaled for the check. "I'm sorry to be so abrupt, but to get you in on that audition for Friday, I need to make a few calls. Here, lunch is on me," Bud said, dropping cash on the table, and standing up to leave.

*   *   *

Bud came through and Livy headed back to New York at the end of the week for the recording session. Crossing Washington Square Park, he entered a weird cyclone of humanity, strolling past bucket drummers and break dancers spinning on cardboard, the smells of African incense and carbonized pretzel, mixed with the smell of the underground coming through the grates. He entered 15 Waverly Place and went upstairs to the Sound Lab. Livy sat down in the waiting area next to a guy wearing giant dark glasses with his nose buried in *Cosmopolitan*. He looked familiar. Then they called the man, "Pee-wee, you're next."

That was all Livy had to hear. He could care less about whatever he did a decade ago. He was mad at Pee-wee for trying to steal his bread and butter.

Not long after Pee-wee departed, Livy, last in line, stepped to the microphone just as the producer behind the glass began: "So this is the background. The former count got too soft over the years. He lost the cape, filed the fangs and lost the kids. Don't do hip or cool. The only way to get these kids' attention is to scare the poop out of them. So instead of reading the whole script, we're going to read the obligatory scene at the end of the commercial where we cut to the complete breakfast shot—a bowl of cereal pictured with a glass of orange juice and toast. Imagine the count adding milk to his bowl of Vampire Bites as you're reading the lines. Yes, got it? This is where we scare the kids and satisfy the lawyers by adding milk. Okay, rolling."

Livy widened his eyes and read the script in his best-clipped Transylvanian: "Vampire Bites cereal scares up a monstrous appetite, part of a complete breakfast for over one thousand years." Then he let out a blood-curdling scream. Livy looked up when he finished reading it. "How was that? Scary enough for you?"

"You can go over the top. You have max headroom."

After a few more takes, the client and the producer were finally satisfied.

*   *   *

The front of the barn where Jessie lived was almost entirely open to the view of the river. The barn doors had been replaced by clear glass French doors. When Livy came up the steps, the motion detector kicked on, and the light alarmed Jessie, until she recognized Livy's form. She slid open the door but stood there guarding the entrance.

"You're ... still selling the house?"

"To the contrary, I have good news. May I come in and share it with you? Would you like to hear it? You'll be happy."

Jessie stood aside for Livy to enter. "I heard you were in New York auditioning?"

"I'm fresh back from the studio. These clients are getting pickier and pickier. I can tell from their expressions that they don't really know what they're doing. Anyway, when I was on the train upstate, my agent texted and gave me the good news. After months of auditioning, the client liked my voice the best."

"And you were auditioning for?"

"The spokesman for Vampire Bites cereal."

"A perfect fit."

Livy rolled his eyes. "It's like a lobster trap. Once you go to cartoon land you never come back. Clients peg you forever."

"Sounds like just what you deserve."

The original ladder to the hayloft was still in place. The fragrance of the two-hundred-year-old hickory posts and beams reminded Livy of Valentine's wine cellar and its rows of nineteenth-century sherries. Jessie sat him down at the twelve-foot dining table made from the old barn doors, now covered with unusual varieties of baby pumpkins, Indian corn, and zucchinis. "You said good news?

"I've come to some clarity about Burleighwood. I want to commit to this place. I pulled the house from the market an hour ago. I used to think that it was the people that mattered, not the old house. Well, it's still about the people," Livy said, looking Jessie directly into her eyes. "Just now that my uncle is gone, this place has taken on new meaning. I broke my own rules," Livy said, breaking into his new character's voice, "I decided being a vampire was not so bad. Darling, I think you can now *count* on me."

She laughed. "You're funny."

Livy then cut his normal voice. "The residuals coming in from the count will keep the house in the family, and next week I'm auditioning for the voice of a rabbit."

"Rabbits? Those turbo rodents eat my lettuce."

Livy Wrinkled his nose. "Cartoons don't eat lettuce."

Jessie's eyes lit up. "What happened to you? Won't the count hurt your career?"

"No, I just wish changing my life was as easy as changing voice."

Jessie looked at him long and hard. "You're doing fine."

"But everyone still hates me."

"It's time to make friends. You can start with me."

Livy leaned into her lips. It was a soft, soulful kiss. The river of time had gone retrograde. Bad feelings vanished from Livy's body. As their lips parted, they held hands like two young lovers and slowly made their way upstairs to her bed. Livy kissed her, and she pressed closer. He reached behind and unzipped her sundress, which fell to the floor.

Livy awakened to bliss circulating in his body. He hardly wanted to move. Jessie had already gone to her fields, and Livy lay there in languid bliss. His body, now well loved, imported itself to the bathroom. He was greeted by the fragrance of oatmeal soap and Bergamot. He had missed the little details and the richness of daily life that women insist on, and which bachelors live without. Afterwards, Livy descended the ladder. He stood in the center of her great room and turned a full circle taking in all of Jessie. No sign of Laura Ashley or Martha Stewart.

The walls were covered with the yet-to-be-discovered artists of the New York underground. Bookshelves lined both sides of the fireplace—Plato, Plutarch and, wedged between them, Pynchon's *Gravity's Rainbow* held its unlikely place. Even with her Vassar education, Jessie was a born farmer from Wisconsin. The faux farm-to-table folks from the city had never seen a cow much less milked one.

On his walk home, as he passed Tad's barn, he poked his head in the door.

"Hey," Tad said, "the car's almost ready. It may even get you to California."

"Well, maybe I won't be driving that car to California anymore."

"It will definitely get you to Jessie's loft and back." Tad winked.

CHAPTER 17

Crum Elbow is full of crooks and crannies, but there are still pockets of paradise, if you know where to look.

—Valentine Hitch, *Crook's Paradise*

L ivy was starting to understand the gift to the welfare of the community that Valentine saw in the Spotted Cow. This ski hill had been Valentine's last bequest to the youth of Crum Elbow. Not only had he envisioned a new rope tow, he had also provided the funds to run the ski lift in perpetuity. Livy realized that as much as Valentine wanted to bring back the Spotted Cow ski hill, he was even more interested in creating a sanctuary.

Valentine hoped that no matter how much the town fathers despoiled the sides of the roads and the commercial world told children that they have to buy all kinds of junk to be happy, the youth of Crum Elbow would never lose touch with the "simple pleasure of gliding down a hill after a snowstorm," as Valentine used to say.

Livy knew he couldn't do it alone. He needed backup. He needed a band. He needed Jessie. She was his Beethoven in the garden, eighty-eight keys to her kingdom. Tad on bass and Hollis Dixon on drums. Valentine's Burleighwood Band. One late summer night, with the smell of autumn already in the air, the fab four convened around the mahogany dining table. Livy raised his glass to the merry transcendentalists. "Here's to fulfilling Valentine's directive."

Like a good bass player, Tad intuited Livy. "I knew there had to be a catch."

The slow shuffle beat of Hollis kept time.

"We're all here by Valentine's grace," Livy said, pointing to a black-and-white photograph of Valentine on the mantle, posing with his seven-foot skis. "Valentine wanted to create a place free of lawyers and regulators, safe from the creepy part of our culture. He wanted local families to be able to get away from insurance waivers. Valentine wanted to create a pastoral alternative."

Hollis was confused. "What about all that land along the river he gave away. Doesn't the Emerald Necklace qualify?"

"You won't be able to build anything taller than a park bench once the Green Border regulations take effect," said Livy.

Jessie had been skiing since she was three years old. When Valentine told her his dream for the Spotted Cow, she went and checked it out. It was so overgrown. If Jessie hadn't found the remnants of the rope tow, she wouldn't have found the ski hill.

"All I know is every time it snows, Jessie treks up the hill with skins on her skis to the top. She don't need no rope tow," Tad said, admiring. He was the Burleigh in Burleighwood.

"Yes, well, Jessie is special. She can fly. Anyway, we have work to do. That's why you're so important to this project, Tad," Livy said.

"Don't worry, I can get us a bulldozer," Tad reassured the group. He looked at Jessie.

"Did you bring the wine?"

Jessie nodded. "Yes, please help yourself."

Livy continued. There was a quickening of the slow shuffle. "This place could be crawling with park rangers soon, so you're going to have to ease up on the Sour Diesel. Got that, Mister Tad?"

"Ease on the deez. Done deal."

His glibness did not sit well with Jessie. She could smell a skunk. "Do you mind if I blaze?" Tad asked.

Livy, the Californian, consented. "Sure, Tad. Let us know when you've found the sweet spot."

Tad pulled a joint out of his wallet and sparked it. "What's next?" Tad inquired with an exhale.

Hollis loved a second-hand high. "How about an ashtray, Tad?" he said, concerned about the antique rug.

"When was the last time you skied, Livy?" Jessie asked.

"Not since my whole family went downhill."

"Funny. Well, remember to grab onto the rope tow and don't let go of that thing," Jessie said.

The following week, Tad's friend, Aldo, rolled up the dirt farm road in a cloud of dust with his great big Caterpillar in tow. The heavy, unwieldy rig had almost taken out one of Burleighwood's historic gateposts and had left tire imprints in the soft lawn as it meandered up the driveway. Within an hour, Tad and Aldo were crunching and crushing a new path through the woods, full-on Lewis and Clark. Snap! Crackle! Pop! The bulldozer was making breakfast of the forest floor. Tad shouted at Aldo and let out a "yee-haw!" as they bounced wildly up and down in the cab, ducking whipping branches and leaving a plume of black smoke and angry yellow jackets in their wake.

Hollis headed west across the Mid-Hudson River Bridge into a red sun. He had read in a local newspaper that the Bonticou ski area was closing down, and everything from the rental equipment to the picnic tables from the lodge were being sold. He had an appointment with the owner, who had run Bonticou for the last fifty years.

Hollis pulled up into the empty lot off Mountain Rest Road and entered the lodge, a two-story, rough-hewn log building with a huge stone fireplace. The room was filled with hickory furniture and memorabilia; the walls were covered with black-and-white photographs of the lodge dating back to 1954. Hollis was greeted by the smell of a pipe. He called out to the owner, who stood at the opposite end of the lodge. "Hello. How are you? I'm Hollis Dixon. You must be Frank Valentino."

Frank walked toward him with hand extended. "Nice to meet you," he said cheerily in a gruff smoker's voice.

"I've been coming up for years, but I never stopped here."

"You ski?"

"No. I have a hard-enough time walking on snow and ice."

"Just curious. I don't ski either, and I own a ski hill."

"I'm helping a friend bring a historic ski run back to life. It's just a small hill. It has a rope tow, but it's decrepit. We wanted to provide free skiing for the kids of the community. My friend, Valentine, thought they needed to get away from their screens—he wanted them to have a place to go outside and get some fresh air. I read in the local papers that you were closing and saw your ad in the PennySaver."

"Did you come to pick up the rope, or if not, I'd be happy to deliver it?"

"But we haven't talked price yet."

"Just tell me when and where. We'll deliver it. I'll send a couple of extra men to install it."

"Slow down, Frank. What is this going to set me back?"

"It's my pleasure to donate it."

"No cost?"

"This one is on me, chief. I want to support you and your friend. I'm closing, but the kids coming up today need all the fresh air they can get."

CHAPTER 18

The value in our heritage continues to unfold, but it takes more than a village. It takes context to link the past with the future.

—Valentine Hitch, *Crook's Paradise*

Livy had asked Jessie to join him at the big house to meet with Emmett to grok his river data. While waiting for him, they settled into the wicker with tea in the presence of tall trees. Black Locusts had been planted around the house in the nineteenth century as natural lightning rods. "These are amazing trees," Jessie said.

"This place seems to attract lightning," Livy noted.

"It certainly struck Winks," Jessie said.

"That cat was bold: national TV, running for mayor, all while he was a wanted felon. What was he thinking?"

"I'm sure he'd done this before," Jessie said.

"Well, how about Flintlock?" Livy asked.

"Now there's mystery inside a conundrum. She's probably a criminal, too, highly principled but corrupt."

"Do you think that's her real name?"

Jessie laughed. "It's beyond me."

Emmett wheeled down the driveway on his ten-speed, carefully missing the potholes and joined them on the porch. "Emmett, meet Jessie."

The young man reached out and shook Jessie's hand. "Emmett Stone."

"Jessie Chandler. I'm delighted and enchanted."

"How's my favorite hydrologist?" Livy said, welcoming him with a hug.

"I still find it hard to believe that Livy picked you up hitchhiking on the Continental Divide," Jessie said.

"Yup, I caught a ride all the way."

"Curious how life works. I had no idea I was fetching the new river doctor," Livy said.

"What does the river doctor do?" Jessie asked.

"I track the pollution and its perpetrators."

"I saw Emmett on the news when Winks's plane went down," Livy said.

"I saw that guy out flying his seaplane every day," Emmett said.

'What surprises me is that they never found his body. That's pretty unusual. Bodies bloat and float until they're eaten," Livy said.

"From where I was standing, I didn't see a pilot in that plane. My guess is that he put it on autopilot," Emmett said.

"That's the first explanation that makes any sense. The crash seemed too convenient," Jessie said.

"Winks is a pro. This is what he does. It's a pattern, with Flintlock in cahoots," Emmett said.

"Well, why didn't you go to the police?" Livy asked Emmett.

"I was more concerned with what Grubb was dumping in the river," Emmett said and unrolled a map and stretched it out like canvas. Livy scrutinized it and realized that Emmett had documented every rill, kill, creek, all with Dutch names, running into the waters of the Hudson at Crum Elbow.

"Your neighbor turned the ice boat camp into a toxic waste dump," Emmett explained. "There was a continuous flow of dump trucks filled to the brim with nasty shit like Benzene, acid tar waste, and some gnarly carcinogens from construction renovations and old gas stations. It's a lot cheaper for Grubb's operation to quietly dump it in the river than pay to remediate it in his industrial corridor in South Jersey. Unfortunately, even *Crook's brook* is polluted."

"Grubb belongs in jail," Livy declared.

"I don't normally think of a hydrologist as a crime fighter," Jessie said.

"Think about it. It all comes down to forensics. Where there's toxic waste, there's usually a crime."

"Are you armed?" Jessie asked.

"I don't need weapons," Emmett said. "I gathered enough information to put the Grubb family in jail for two lifetimes. This has now gone all the way to Washington. Homer Junior and his son are going to jail. That's what happens when a billionaire with brains gets involved."

"Can you tell us who?" Livy asked.

"No, he's a behind-the-scenes kind of guy. He's not out for glory. He's more interested in redemption."

"The tide has turned," Jessie said, looking at Livy.

"Now Crumwold Hall should be protected so the whole town can enjoy it," Livy said.

"Livy, you might want to check in with the Hitch Foundation. If anyone cares about the future of Crumwold Hall, they should," Jessie said.

"Well, the current board members are my generation. I know half of them from boarding school. Maybe one of them will be at the fundraiser next week. Hopefully, they have fond memories of the Elbow," Livy said, grimacing. The last thing Livy wanted to do was put on a coat and tie. By the standards of the old rules, he had become a sartorial horror.

"Jessie, are you up for a trip to New York next week?"

"Sure, but isn't this a reunion for you?"

"Yes, with you."

"Would you come with me to see Ground Zero? I lost my friend Kevin Connors there," Jessie said, sounding sad.

"I had a chance once to go down there, but I passed. Sure, let's do that."

When the day of the fundraiser arrived, Livy consulted Valentine's closet for suitable attire to confront the family mythologies. After living in California, the necktie was an alien object. He was pleased and delighted to find that Valentine's clothes fit him so well. The seersucker anachronism and white bucks, the poplin jacket and blue and white gingham shirt, the khakis and classic blue blazer with shiny brass buttons—classic boarding school, categorically out—they were all too familiar. He was no longer any of these people, and he was all of these people. He decided to keep the California cowboy jeans and hiking boots and go with a white shirt with French cuffs, coat, and tie. He settled on a skinny, black four-in-hand tie that was so old school it was now new. He looked at himself in the floor mirror and saw the story of his life: mountain man on the bottom and preppy on top. Livy had been at Saint James in the late seventies and early eighties when the mossy, tradition-bound institution of learning had become a cauldron of subcultures. The pendulum swung almost over-night. The Deadhead into a dinner jacket. It also didn't hurt that Livy was a Hitch. Sometimes, the name provided self-assurance, particularly at St. James, where his ancestors were still revered.

Since he was planning to see his brother Archie, Livy stopped off in his bedroom and pocketed a little red football that was loaded with associations. In a supreme act of muscle memory, he grabbed both banisters and vaulted the last four or five steps, as he'd done when he was a young monkey of twelve.

Jessie was waiting in her truck at the lawn circle to drive them to the train. She wore a quick-zip black dress.

Livy came down from the front steps looking like a Hitch, well, by the old rules, half-Hitch. "Nice duds," Jessie hollered. Her eyes traveled down the seam and marveled at his hiking boots and jeans as Livy hopped into the car. "The outfit is crazy."

"It's my way of finding a balance. I love the little black dress; you look like a runway model."

Livy got in. Jessie chuckled, nodded in agreement, and off they headed to the Poughkeepsie train station. They boarded the 12:50 Metro-North and arrived in New York two hours later.

Livy took Jessie's hand and navigated their way through a crowd and up the marble steps of Grand Central Station. They emerged on Vanderbilt Avenue across from the Yale Club and hailed a cab to Battery Park.

She took a deep breath. She had been postponing going to Ground Zero for almost four years. Livy still couldn't get over the big gaping space in the sky where the towers had been. It was a sickening feeling.

The pictures of those lost had been taken down. Vendors were selling cheap trinkets made in China: American flags, key chains, Statues of Liberty, and commemorative freedom coins. Anything to make a buck, crap that was supposed to be worth something one day.

Jessie stood behind the fence and gaped into the abyss as she replayed the day in her head. She had been meeting with an art restorer in Long Island City when all the bridges and tunnels closed, and she had to walk across the Queensboro Bridge to get back into the city. She looked down in the hole and then up at the sky. "Goodbye, Kevin, sleep with the angels."

"I'm sure I knew someone," Livy whispered. "Many of my old Princeton classmates worked on Wall Street."

After a moment of reverence, they hailed a cab and headed uptown. "How often do you get to New York?" Livy asked.

"I go in to check on my restaurant accounts. I meet with the owners and the chefs."

"Really, you're selling into Manhattan?"

"My timing was right. People are becoming more aware of where their food is coming from, and they're horrified by it. During the growing season, the menus in New York City shift to a greater variety of vegetables from local farmers. It's the only time that the Hudson Valley can compete with California."

The Hitchcock family lived in a penthouse on Fifth Avenue. Livy presented the doorman the invitation for the Saint James's School reception.

The doorman looked down at Livy's climbing boots before holding the door open and escorting him and Jessie to the private gold-leaf-and-mahogany elevator, along with several other people.

The elevator door opened into the family's apartment, which was the width and length of the building and stretched for half a block. The host, wearing their Alma mater's red and blue school tie, a blue blazer, and gray flannels, greeted them as they stepped out of the elevator. They walked past a Picasso and Matisse and into the gin of the crowd. Attractive young catering staff, balancing smoked salmon and cucumber-dill tea sandwiches nimbly navigated clustering alumni. Livy deftly lifted two champagne flutes from the tray of a chiseled young waiter cruising by and handed one to Jessie. They then found a place to stand when Livy was spotted by Mr. Alumni himself, bow-tied Peter Stafford.

"Well, look who's here? Long Lost Livingston. I'm class secretary, so I happen to know we haven't heard from you since you left, right after graduation."

Livy shook his second-cousin's hand. "I live on the West Coast, Peter."

"Did you know that Arthur Phelps died in Tower One?"

"Shit," Livy said, reeling from a direct hit to his heart. "Did Art have a family?"

"Wife and two children. We had a big fundraiser for the family."

"Good work, Peter. Meet my dear friend, Jessie."

"Great to meet you, Jessie. You came home again, Livy?"

"Yup, like Candide, I came home to tend my own garden. Since I've been back at Burleighwood, I've been reading the family foundation newsletter. I see that you're the new chairman," Livy said.

"John Winthrop Hitch's capital has gone global. Our scholarship students come from all over the planet," Peter added proudly.

"I may have a candidate for you."

"I'd be happy to meet any candidate of yours, Livy."

"You know him."

"Was he at Saint James with us?"

"Sort of, certainly during some very pleasant vacations from school. I want to recommend Crumwold Hall. It's for sale."

"You're confusing me. These scholarships are for people."

"I realize that, Peter. But I think we need to include Crumwold Hall in our mission."

"My family was part of Crum Elbow. It was a sinking ship for us," Peter said.

"John Winthrop's foundation was set up to help the people of Crum Elbow," Livy reminded.

"Look, Liv. It's not happening. Don't push it. We're way beyond spending John Winthrop's money."

"I'm sorry to hear that. Well, I guess I'll have to depend on the kindness of strangers."

"You're living in the past, my friend. You're fighting a losing battle. The cultural migration for the last sixty years has been moving east of the Hudson, or toward the Hamptons, not up river. Crumwold Hall has outlived its era."

From where Livy was standing, he spotted the back of his brother's head in the far corner of the room. Livy was glad to see Archie still had a full head of hair. "Nice catching up with you, Peter."

"Sorry to disappoint you Livy, but you were the first to abandon Crum Elbow."

"I didn't forsake Crum Elbow. I left my family."

"Is there a difference?" Peter asked, keeping the pressure on.

Livy didn't deign a response. There was an awkward silence. He looked over at Jessie.

Jessie stepped forward and shook Peter's hand. "So nice to meet you, Peter."

Jessie took a sip of champagne as Peter walked off to drink more Kool-Aid. "Was Peter at Princeton with you?"

"No, he was among the first generation in his family who didn't get in. By the time we came along, your family name no longer guaranteed admittance. In fact, it could even have worked against Peter."

"How did you get in?"

"I had the grades."

"I'm sorry your cousin wasn't more helpful."

"Times have changed. People who should care, don't."

Jessie followed Livy across the room. Livy put his hand on his brother's shoulder. Archie turned, and their eyes met. There was a surge of recognition and an awkward embrace.

"You good?" Archie asked.

"Yes, I'm well," Livy replied. "You?"

"Hanging in there. It sure is good to see you, Liv!"

"I'm with you," Livy said, clapping his older brother on the back as they separated. "Archie, meet Jessie."

"A joy and a pleasure."

"Sorry to hear about Valentine," Archie said, turning back to Livy.

"Well, Valentine will really never die. Let's go for a walk."

"Sounds like a great idea. The park is across the street."

The three entered Central Park at Seventy-Second Street. Livy reached into his pocket and produced the miniature red football. "Check this out. When was the last time you saw this?"

"Valentine gave me that," Archie said, his eyes brightening as he suddenly turned and broke into his favorite pattern and button-hooked left. He turned around just as the ball spiraled into his hands.

From the speeding train rumbling north, Livy gazed at the ebb and flow of the Hudson. He must have ridden this same train to Poughkeepsie hundreds of times. He recalled all the different people he had thought he had been. But, this train ride he felt different. He looked at Jessie, and she smiled back. He had always felt like he was visiting in the places he'd lived, no matter how long he stayed. His brain finally relaxed.

*   *   *

The next morning, Livy brewed coffee and headed out to the porch to sip it. He was still smarting from Proud Peter's disconnect with Crumwold Hall and Crum Elbow. Suddenly, from the porch, he saw a cherry-red, 1950s Cadillac, replete with shark-style fins, coming up the driveway. Livy had gotten used to tourists, lone-wolf photographers, and seekers of lost worlds ignoring the *No Trespassing* signs at the entrance to Burleighwood. It had become a form of drive-by history for some people to make a quick pass up the driveway and around the lawn circle to get a glimpse of the historic house, then cruise back down the driveway and out the main entrance before anyone noticed. But the car pulled right up to the front entrance. Livy set down his coffee and approached the driver.

"Let me introduce myself. I'm Rupert Obermeyer, but you can call me Obie. Even my mother called me Obie."

"I'm Livingston Hitch, but you can call me Livy."

"I'm really sorry about Valentine. I had just gotten to know him."

"I'm his nephew. How did you guys meet?"

"As Chicken Charlie's CEO, I set up shop across from all that Roosevelt history. Valentine woke my ass up. He made me see how dang out of place our roof chicken looked across from Franklin Roosevelt's favorite Oak tree. You get to my age and you start thinking, 'What was I thinking?' Our conversation was like being hit on the head by a two-by-four."

"He must have hit you pretty damn hard."

"Hard enough to remove my blinders. I was in a fantasy growth bubble, envisioning Chicken Charlies everywhere, but I wasn't thinking about the environment. I had no idea how much I was heating up the planet with our big ass balance sheet. After Valentine's wake up call, I went back to our board. Seeing I had been radicalized and no longer their boy, they dropped me like a hot chicken burger, ousted me from the company I founded, like Steve Jobs. I tried to fight the board over the size of the roof chicken. I didn't realize we were competing with the Golden Arches, and that's when I met Emmett, the hydrologist, who told me that he caught a ride with you all the way from the Continental Divide."

"Ahhh, so you're the billionaire who helped Emmett put Grubb in jail?"

"By that time, Emmett was already very well acquainted with the crooks in Crum Elbow. When I picked him up, Emmett pointed out that our roof chicken was pocket change compared with Grubb's footprint. Picking Emmett up hitchhiking was like picking up a new catalytic converter for my Caddy."

CHAPTER 19

It's reassuring that goodness is still at work rumbling its way through our history.

—Valentine Hitch, *Crook's Paradise*

When Valentine's book rolled off the presses into the collective mind, it included the photograph of Grubb 3.0's futon and PC in the tower, which had taken on much greater meaning now that Grubb Junior and 3.0 were in jail, and the crooks had been ejected from Crumwold Hall. Ed Williams disappeared into Miami. Whoever Emerson Winks was—that character was never seen again, but his story became suburban legend. After several phone calls that the authorities later tracked to Tennessee, Jillian Flintlock vanished as well. She was last seen at Paulette's green dry cleaner.

Hollis had been monitoring Valentine's book sales, and Livy had agreed to meet him at a pier on the river. "I have something I want to show you," Hollis said.

Livy approached a wooden pallet with waterlogged boxes baptized by the Hudson.

"What is all this?"

"It's a pallet of your uncle's books found submerged off Crum Elbow Point. *Crook's Paradise* was selling like hot cakes—expensive, hardcover hotcakes at $29.95 a pop—but, apparently, a lot of books were also flying off the shelves and into the river. A clear case of sabotage."

"Valentine's book is obviously threatening all the right people. The Grubbs may be in jail and the neighborhood safer, but no doubt the corruption continues."

The following morning, Livy opened his eyes and took in the hickory beams. The sheets were flannel, and he could smell the fragrance of gardenia. Rolling to his left, he pressed closer to Jessie from behind and kissed the nape of her neck. Jessie opened her eyes, turned over, and snuggled into his chest. They lay entwined in stillness. For the next hour, they drifted in and out of deep-woods bliss.

Then, Jessie whispered in his ear. "I have an idea." Livy opened his eyes and gazed at the ceiling.

"We could easily become a dairy farm. I just researched it. All we need are eight cows to qualify for the dairy subsidy. We can cut our taxes by nearly half."

"Wow, seriously? That would be a big help."

"I had another idea."

"I hope it's as good as the first one," Livy chuckled.

"The Grubbs and mall are gone. How about we deliver Crook's Paradise to every mailbox and mail slot in Crum Elbow."

"Well, about two hundred books are waterlogged beyond recognition, but Hollis figures we have about eight hundred that are readable," Livy said.

"Well, since we're not charging for them, they don't have to be perfect. How long do you think it will take?"

"It's a big job, stopping and delivering at each house," Livy said.

"Yup, if it were a newspaper, we could throw it on the front lawn. Still, I want to give it to them personally."

Jessie's resolve impressed Livy. "I'm Paul Revere ready to ride and spread the alarm through every village and farm. But do you think anyone will read it, let alone heed Valentine's message?"

"Wow, such optimism," Jessie said, frowning.

"Valentine was hoping to solve a problem that most folks don't have time to think about," Livy reasoned.

"We may as well go back to sleep," Jessie said, rolling over.

"I'm sorry to be so negative." Livy was talking to the skylight. "Most people are just trying to get by. Caring about the view is a luxury. Do you think the kid making minimum wage, who walks home from work on Route 9, cares about the view?"

"Well, maybe if he did care, we'd be living in a different world," Jessie said. Livy and Jessie chose to start with the homes on Mansion Drive. They loaded the back seat of the truck with boxes of books. Then, they set off in a cloud of dust. With gravity pulling them to the left, Livy swung a hard right into Mansion Drive. The neighborhood was already in transition. Many of the old immigrant stock were flocking to Florida or dying off, and their children were not returning to Crum Elbow after college. Some worked for the very same corporations destroying Smallville, America. Crum Elbow's newcomers were as likely to be Indian or Asian rather than the old immigrant groups like the Italians and the Irish. As always in

America, assimilation had become all about modifying everything to fit in, sort of like Superman becoming Clark Kent.

They proceeded to pollinate the neighborhood, going door to door. An hour into their delivery, they still had not encountered a single human being. Valentine's book made its way into mailboxes and slots, under windshield wipers, and on door steps. Cosmo and his wife were the first to answer their door.

"Jessie, what you got here?"

"It's Valentine's book. We want everyone in Crum Elbow to read it." Cosmo looked up and smiled at the brightest star in the sky. In death, Valentine had become his supernova.

At the dead-end of Mansion Street, they were confronted with what looked like a UFO mother ship that had landed in the Crumwold woods. Upon closer inspection, they found Crumwold Hall lit up like a river boat. The chains had been removed from the entrance gates, and Obie's shark-finned red Caddy was heading out of the driveway. He rolled down his window and smiled."Nice to see you again, Livy, and who may I have the pleasure of meeting?"

"Hi Obie, I'm Jessie Chandler. Livy's told me all about you. We're passing out copies of Valentine's book."

"This may surprise you, but I've already read it. I had no idea saving the Elbow could be so much fun."

The sight of the mansion blazing left Jessie feeling bewildered. "Did you buy Crumwold Hall?"

"Yup, took it right out of Grubb's grubby hands. My accountant would prefer if I stayed in Florida, but, as you may know, Emmett and I are now a team. He's used to tiny budgets and begging for grants. His grant writing days are over. Let's just say he's fully funded for life. Emmett's the son I never had. He really walks the talk. He considers cars the bane of the planet. I'm the dreamer, Emmett is *Peter-practical*. He's really got the ball rolling. We want to reverse the damage of idiot-growth, my former religion. Our first project is digging up that wasteland of parking lots along Route 9. Emmett says we're uncovering the soil because it needs to breathe. I didn't realize soil is a carbon catcher like Emmett."

"You picked up a hitchhiker and your life changed. Classic," Jessie said.

"Turns out he wasn't just any hitchhiker," Obie said.

"How's Crumwold Hall fit into your plan?" Livy asked Obie.

"The Hall is really more for my education project. I want to see if I can fulfill Valentine's impossible dream of restoring Crum Elbow. The goal is to reclaim the grounds of FDR's Springwood, Crumwold Hall, and Burleighwood, and then recreate Crum Elbow as it once was. And that's just phase one. The town has been bulldozing Roosevelt for way too long. But, mum's the word. Remember, I'm a behind-the-scenes guy. I put up the money," said the unlikely prophet in his big red pile of a car. Obie looked down at his watch, "I'm late for dinner, but the door is open. Please feel free to look around."

"We don't want to intrude," Jessie said.

"Oh, I don't live here. This is a big, empty house, and I want to keep it that way for now. I'm late, but I'm so glad we met, Jessie," Obie said.

"The feeling is mutual, Obie. When are we going to see you next?" Jessie asked.

"Let's talk before I leave tomorrow for New York?" he said with a wave as the great, red boat sailed off through the gateposts.

"Well, finally the good guys have captured the tower. Let's go check it out," Jessie said.

"What's the deal with towers?" Livy asked.

"Control freaks love towers. They love being above the fray so they can hit you with boiling oil. It's medieval, pure evil. Have you ever actually been up there before?" Jessie asked.

"We used to play baseball on the south lawn. By the time our interest turned to the house, the Jesuits had gone, and we couldn't get anywhere near the house."

They headed toward the door. Jessie had heard about Colonel Rogers's Gatsby-sized New Year's Eve parties but hadn't quite realized how huge the entrance hall was. Crumwold Hall's memories had faded as the wood darkened. Old daguerreotypes, photographs, deeds, wills, maps, and a precious trove of documents, containing the entire history of Crum Elbow, had been accumulating in the darkened alcove of the entrance to the hall. Livy found himself staring at a book of illustrations he'd found atop a large stack of early-twentieth-century books. He leafed through the book and marveled at a photograph of FDR sitting in an uncomfortable-looking wooden chair with heavy metal braces on his legs at a New Year's party in the great hall.

"Wow, there's a strange feeling here. It's a little scary," Jessie said.

"So ... this is what happens to these places. They end up as these strange museums that nobody goes to," Livy said.

"I guess this happens when the families die off and their big country places outlive them."

"Yeah, sort of like an abandoned tortoise shell. I wonder what the sound is like in here?" Livy yodeled. "Great acoustics."

The ground-floor public rooms looked magnificent, and it didn't take much of an imagination to conjure up better times in the great hall. Livy looked up at the cracked ceilings, "That's serious water damage. Where's the love?"

"It's a good thing this place is Maine granite. If it were clapboard, all the local critters would have moved in by now," Jessie observed.

After wandering around the main floor in a state of wonder, Livy said, "Let's go upstairs."

"Is that the way to the tower?"

"I think so. Let's check it out," Livy said. The iron steps spiraled up into the tower. Jessie marveled, "Look at this iron work, we may as well be in New Orleans. How many steps do you think there are, Livy?"

"Twenty-five, maybe thirty."

"No. It's more than that. Let's count."

They counted their way up, "...thirty-five, thirty-six, thirty-seven, thirty-eight." Jessie reached the top step. "Thirty-nine steps, just like the Hitchcock movie."

They entered through the tower door and imbibed the room. Jessie walked over to the window and stood in the light of magnified moon that cast her shadow on the wall. She may as well have been the goddess Athena, the wise counselor of Odysseus.

She turned and looked back at Livy. The spell was cast. When Livy dropped down on one knee and held out his hand, Jessie came over and grasped both of his hands. "I can't think of a better time or even a better place to ask you this. Jessie, will you marry me?"

"Livy…" Jessie said, her mind arrested.

"It's never been clearer. We were meant to be together. Will you marry me, Jessie?"

Jessie said yes first with her eyes, and then with her whispered word, "Yes."

Livy stood up, and they kissed in the moonlight.

CHAPTER 20

Crum Elbow is out of the history making business. The takers have replaced the givers and sold us the rope we're hanging ourselves from.

—Valentine Hitch, *Crook's Paradise*

Valentine's book, which had started off as rearguard action involving bulldozers, had become a baton that he had handed off to a billionaire in a generational relay. Valentine's book had become a ball of light in Obie's hands. He realized that it was naïve to think the local politicians were going to solve the problem. They weren't even aware of the problem. As far as they were concerned, there was no problem. The only hope for the town was the bulldozer.

Jessie led the way up the fieldstone steps from her place. Livy's muscles remembered them perfectly, although the steps had sunk deeper into the earth since his youth. Jessie stopped and turned to look at Livy, "I've been thinking about Obie and that red boat of a car of his."

"He's the dude of the moment, Winks cubed."

"Winks didn't have the clout. Now Flintlock was another story. She wore the pants. Too bad, with all that talent, she and Winks turned out to be more like Bonnie and Clyde," Jessie added.

"Feels like Obie came down from the mountain with tablets," Livy said.

As they nearly reached Tad's barn, the air was alive with the horn section of the Dukes of Dixieland. Then the music stopped. In the distance, they could see Tad and Hollis talking to Obie. Tad then circled Obie's car and bent down and checked out the super-glide suspension of the 1960 Cadillac Coupe De Ville. "Wow, now this is an example of pre-plastic, guzzler engineering, flies like an iron butterfly."

Livy approached and called out. "I heard the horns. I knew it must be the king."

"But no longer of the house of chicken."

"Obie, I see your license plates still say CACKLE," Jessie teased.

"It reminds me of what a joke my life used to be, when I had chicken burgers on the brain."

"Well, Jessie and I have good news. We're getting married," Livy said, feeling more at ease than ever.

"Congratulations, Livy, it's about time," Hollis said. "Valentine would approve."

"Well, you're a great team," Obie said as he got out of the car.

"Yup, good thing your car ended up in the lake or you might have missed the boat," Tad remarked.

"What's your plan?" Jessie asked.

"I'm picking up where Valentine left off. I guess the only difference is I'm using my bank account to set in motion forces that protect Crum Elbow's great American heritage from cagey developers like myself, at least what's left of it."

"You're our hero, Obie," Jessie said.

"We all know how long being a hero lasts in this country," Obie said, laughing.

Livy wholeheartedly agreed with Jessie. "But you saved Crumwold Hall."

"Not just the Hall, we're rebooting Crum Elbow while we're at it. Instead of inheriting a suburban wasteland, the Crum Elbow High School class of 2045 will inherit the earth, or at least part of Crum Elbow. We're hitting rewind. Let the undoing begin. Check this out," Obie said, opening his trunk, reaching inside and pulling out a map of Crum Elbow assembled from aerial photographs. He unfurled the map on the hood of his car.

"Are those satellite shots?" Hollis asked.

"No, Winks took these from his plane. This is the roadmap to the future he left behind on his desk. Our plan extends out twenty-five years. Back to the bucolic. I'm here to *un-develop*. But truth be told, I'm doing all this for the next generation. I'm not expecting old dogs to learn new tricks. The town planning board is still on the take and developing in the wrong direction."

"How I wish Valentine were here to see your new plans unfold," Livy said.

"You'd be surprised how in touch he is," Obie said with a half-smile and gathered everyone around the map. "Check this out. My team has been quietly buying up all of the single-family houses built on the former Rogers's estate after the war."

"Let me get this straight; you want to tear down people's homes?" Jessie asked incredulously.

"Not necessarily. We already have plans to move fifty houses east of the historic district to the former campus of a defunct women's junior college, in which we're redeveloping it as a neighborhood. Most people I've spoken to have come to realize that their houses probably should never have been built on such historic ground as Crum Elbow, but, at the time, those properties were the most affordable ones available. Some are ready to move now, others want Crum Elbow to be restored, but only after they pass, which is fine."

"Isn't that how the Rockefellers restored Williamsburg? They bought up everything incongruent with colonial history and removed it," Livy said.

"Same idea, but in Crum Elbow, it's a stretch to go back to the thirties, much less the Colonial period," Obie said.

"You're just plain ground-breaking," Livy grinned.

"Exactly, my plan is to start ripping up all *superfluous asphalt* by next spring."

"I like the groove of that phrase, superfluous asphalt," Hollis commented.

"Very amusing, Hollis, but, seriously, I'm going to need everyone's help. I can't do this alone. It takes local support and knowledge, especially from anyone who knew Valentine. You have to realize that some of these folks would just as soon have a Chicken Charlie. I'm going to need your help to sell the community on this."

"We'd be honored," Jessie said, looking over at Livy to confirm.

"Just give us the list, and we'll start knocking," Livy agreed.

"You will find your door-to-door campaigning eye-opening. FDR's forgotten man has been forgotten again," Obie said.

"That describes most of America," Livy agreed.

"Yes, right now most of us could really use a trusting fireside chat. All the abuses of public trust FDR tried to prevent have reared their ugly heads yet again. History repeats itself, but this time, it's intentional," Obie said.

"Had no idea we were living in such a bubble." Hollis said.

"Isn't there supposed to be someone in Washington looking out for us?" Livy asked.

"Well, it's more like the opposite. The wrong people get to the top. They call it deregulation like it's a good thing allowing the political and business classes to cozy up and turn the mortgage market into a vast Ponzi. Maybe you'll even meet Helen Ridley going door to door."

"What's Helen's story?" asked Jessie.

"Helen's a top-producing mortgage broker and has been busy signing reverse-mortgage loans based on inflated-home valuations all over town. She isn't even sure which Roosevelt was born in Crum Elbow, Teddy or Franklin."

Obie wouldn't say why, but he insisted everyone pile into his car: there was something they had to see. Hollis and Tad climbed in his couch of a back seat, and Livy and Jessie hopped in front. Obie then aimed his beloved boat of a battleship down the road toward the river pointing out the futures of forest, farm, and gardens.

At the fork in the road, he stopped the car and gestured to a barely discernible road. "You see that road you can't see? It's soon to be upgraded and sloped for drainage."

"I know you're the man with the plan, but who is going to provide helping hands?" Hollis asked.

"The foundation will need teachers. We'll need farmers. Imagine a whole team of forest makers with seeds and shovels. I'm putting the local rough riders to work. They all want to work. They just need an opportunity."

"They just needed someone to believe in them," Hollis said, knowing their plight all too well.

"What about women? How will they be involved?" Jessie asked.

"Worry not, we're putting women in charge," Obie said with the smile. "They'll be upstairs running the show as well as planting. I don't think most of our male recruits quite realize they'll be entering a woman's world."

"The young men have a harder time growing up around here. Most of them are downwardly mobile. Some escape through the military," Hollis observed.

"They shouldn't have to go to war to become men. I plan to put young men and women to work planting millions of seedlings and native grasses; they can learn to become good stewards of the land," Obie said.

When Obie pulled in front of Tad's shop, Livy leaned over Jessie to shake Obie's hand. "What's your next move?"

Obie paused and rubbed his neck. "More chemo," Obie shouted with a wave as he sailed off down the drive.

"It's curious talking about the future with someone who won't be around to see it. I guess it takes a bulldozer to clear his conscience," Jessie said.

CHAPTER 21

We're seeing the full impact of privileging transient profit and politics over the future.

—Valentine Hitch, *Crook's Paradise*

Summer went into fall. Jessie and Livy made the trip to City Hall and instead of traveling 3,000 miles back to California, Livy moved 600 yards into Jessie's cozy loft. He suggested to Jessie that they take up residence in the manor house together, but it felt a little too old fashioned for her. She preferred windows and light over dark. Livy moved in with an eye toward setting up a recording studio where Valentine had once developed his photographs.

Through much of the fall, doors opened and slammed. Even Obie's signing bonus, and Jessie and Livy's door-to-door charm offensive did not penetrate the resistance. Thanks to the housing bubble, homeowners were quite content with their status quo. But thanks to Tad's persistence, and the precarious nature of the economy, after the crash of 2008, doors began opening.

One afternoon, Livy and Jessie approached a split-level house with a glittering Christmas tree in its picture window. Billy Boy Shear's family had been living the American Dream on Colonel Rogers's polo field since the end of World War II. There was an old Buick Riviera parked out front, the same Buick that Billy Boy had cruised up and down Route 9 during his debauched high school years. Instead of going to college, Billy had secured a job with IBM, which had employed previous generations from their high school graduation nearly to the grave. But halfway through Billy's tenure, manufacturing moved overseas, along with his job. There was nothing left to bolt together. Lifetime employment and gold watches became another fairytale the older generation told their children about how life *used* to be.

Suddenly, the garage door opened, and out came Billy wearing Levi's and a rumpled white shirt. The IBM cowboy handed over a manila envelope. "It's all notarized, just like you wanted, Jessie."

"Thank you, Billy."

"Thanks to you and Livy. You saved my ass."

The whole neighborhood had been pressured to accept "pre-approved" mortgage scams. Most had their life savings invested in their houses. They were lucky that Jessie and Livy had followed behind the mortgage *breakers*, to sit at their kitchen tables, carefully explaining the fine print, which would have taken a lawyer to understand it because they were crafted by lawyers to be confusing.

"Hey, check this out," Billy said, flipping on the garage lights. He pulled a pool cover off his Pathfinder, one of the most storied ice boats on the Hudson."

"Oh my God, the Pathfinder," Livy shouted. "Valentine was likely the last person to take this out on the ice. He went over eighty miles per hour in this antique shell. How did you score this baby?"

"My father discovered it somewhere, probably at an auction. My dad was so excited, but you should have seen my mother's face after she realized she'd lost her parking space in the garage."

"Did your dad race ice boats?" Jessie asked.

"No, he just wanted a piece of river history. He won that one. As you can see, my mother's Buick is still parked under the Maple."

"Wow, I'd give anything to see Uncle Valentine out on the ice again," Livy said wistfully.

A week later, as Christmas approached, Jessie awakened and lay in bed gazing at the ceiling. After a while, she tapped Livy and put her head on his shoulder. "Are you awake?"

Livy grunted. "Yes, I've been lying here missing Valentine. I still can't believe he's really gone."

It had been consistently cold, but there was no snow. The Spotted Cow was barren. On Christmas Eve, an engraved invitation arrived inviting everyone to the first New Year's party at Crumwold Hall in eighty years. Livy thought of Valentine. He couldn't stop thinking of him. Later that day, Livy wound his way through the house, stopped in the study, and climbed the stairs to Valentine's studio. Valentine's absence meant that Christmas was a hole in his heart that desperately needed filling. All of the sudden, Beano came into his mind descending a heavenly staircase.

Livy borrowed Hollis's Jeep for convenience, headed north on Route 9, and finally arrived at the gateposts of Oak Terrace, where Valentine used to visit the spring. He pulled up and parked near Beano's car. Beano was standing guard at Crumwold Hall, even though it was closed for the season. It was a lonely walk to the house. He remembered all the times he had stood with Valentine at the edge of the springs, which were now frozen.

Livy knocked and Beano's face appeared in the window and then opened the door.

"Livy, Merry Christmas, what's up?"

"Merry Christmas to you and your family, Beano," Livy said, then stepped into the foyer. "I have a favor to ask you."

"Sure, fire away."

"I just wanted to ask you again. Did you ever make contact with Valentine?"

"No, but he's been on my mind."

"Do you think he's really dead?"

Beano could see the pain in Livy's eyes. "Well, let's take a moment to be quiet and listen to the universe," Beano said, closing his eyes.

Livy obliged, and after a minute went by, Beano opened his eyes. "From what I can tell, he hasn't reached the other side."

Livy suddenly felt like he'd been given hope. He wasn't sure what kind of hope, but he felt better. He gave Beano a hug. "You just made my Christmas."

Livy headed home with only one thought on his mind. Sliding to a stop at the front entrance, he entered the big house and made his way straight to the study to find the sterling silver cricket cup on the upper shelf. He climbed on a chair and retrieved the cup. He stepped down off the chair, removed the saran wrap cover, and peered into it. Instead of bone fragments, he noticed gold flakes in what all assumed were Valentine's ashes.

CHAPTER 22

In spite of it all, I still believe in America.

—Valentine Hitch, *Crook's Paradise*

On the day before the big New Year's party at Crumwold Hall, as if on cue, twelve inches of fresh snow blanketed everyone's door-step. An hour before the festivities were to begin the following day, Hollis and Tad joined a black-tied Livy for a glass of Valentine's famous lethal eggnog and gingerbread in the kitchen. Tad was clad in his Marine blues. Hollis, who once roamed the world for *Vanity Fair*, had maintained a dinner jacket for special occasions.

Tad sighed, "I'm missing Valentine."

Hollis smiled, "He's right here. I feel him."

"You may be right, Hollis. We not only have crooks; we have disappearing dead guys," Livy added.

"No bodies to speak of," Hollis concurred.

Tad looked confused. A knock at the door and in glided Jessie in her back satin evening gown with jeweled straps and a plunging neckline.

"Don't you look smashing, Jessie," Livy said.

"I'm Madame X tonight. I stepped out of a John Singer Sargent painting for the occasion."

"By any chance, did you bring his Spanish Dancer with you? I could sure use a date," Hollis asked.

"Sorry, Hollis, your beloved dancer now lives in London and is happily remarried."

Tad's eyes popped, then came to rest on Jessie's face. For a brief instant, he saw Jessie as someone other than his tormentor. "Wow, all spruced up."

Jessie smiled and curtsied. "Knocked you for a loop, huh, Tad?" Jessie walked over and straightened Tad's tie.

Although they were gathering to leave, the sound of a large car pulled up to the front door. It could only have been Obie. Livy looked out, "What's our host doing out there?"

Livy went out to meet Obie. As Livy came to the window, he noticed Obie wasn't wearing black-tie and looked depleted. "You're joining us, right?" Livy called out.

"I wish I could but my body has made other plans." Obie literally seemed to be fading, teetering on the edge of time. Obie took a deep breath. "I just want to make one more trip home before I merge into that great river."

"And that would be?" Livy asked.

"Baton Rouge, Louisiana, my Creole belle."

"Have you thought of going to Mexico? They have cancer treatments that have yet to be approved here," Livy said, grasping for something.

"As they say down south, I'm not buying any green bananas. I'm cleared for take-off. Can't say I ain't looking forward to it. Folks who die often come back to life. All you need to understand is that it's all a miracle."

Livy called everyone to the door, and Hollis asked, "What's going on?"

"I think Obie is leaving us."

"What, he's not going to the party?" Jessie said.

Livy said, "No, he's parting, not partying." He leaned into the window. "Wow, you have become one of our founding fathers."

"Maybe a finding father," Obie said, and off he went. They all watched his taillights disappear into the night.

"That man needs a statue in his honor," Tad said.

"Actually, Obie told me that in the end, he wanted to be nobody. In fact, he planned to have 'nobody' written on his tombstone," Livy said.

"What the heck?" said Tad.

"Because there'd be nobody home. He would have merged back into that great river of time."

Shortly afterward, Hollis glided down Crumwold Hall's driveway in four-wheel drive with Jessie in the front seat and Tad and Livy in the back. The weather wasn't an issue because mostly neighbors were invited. Guests began arriving by snowshoes, snowmobile, monster truck, cross-country skis. News of the party had traveled far and wide, even reaching the Colonel's great-granddaughter and once Valentine's cohort Anne Rogers. The mysterious forces of Crum Elbow were back online tugging at the community.

Hollis dropped everyone at the happily lit Crumwold Hall. Strains of Bruce Springsteen and the pulse of the E Street band greeted them as they entered the mansion. Other than the DJ, who had set up his equipment on the landing of the grand stairway, and several other concessions to modernity, Obie had recreated a scene from the hall on New Year's Eve complete with the Christmas tree from Crumwold woods. The fourteen-foot Douglas fir had been topped with a wax angel with gossamer wings, its branches covered with little glass trumpets, glass bells, French dolls, and LED candles. Waiters were serving champagne, sparkling water, hot chocolate, eggnog, and brandy.

The massive fireplace offered a warm respite for cold hands and feet. The hundred families that had once fit into Crumwold Hall on New Year's

Eve and ruled the Empire State from its beginning had been married off and mugged by time. There was nothing gilded about the current hardworking citizens of today's Crum Elbow. Families with surnames like Jurkowski, Miroslav, and Chen now lived in the shadow of Crumwold Hall but hadn't a clue about Colonel Rogers.

"I feel like I'm finally on the right side of history," Livy said, looking to his left and right. He spotted his brother Archie chatting with Billy Shear."

"Wow, I'm having a déjà vu moment; your brother's here," marveled Jessie.

"I think revolution is in the air. Did you get a glass of champagne?"

"Livy, there may be something bubbling in my belly, but it isn't champagne," Jessie said.

For a moment Livy froze. He looked down at Jessie's belly and then into her eyes. She was smiling. Tad elbowed Livy and pointed to Mosley's head bobbing above the crowd.

"Oh my God, it's Mosley…back from British birding," Livy called.

"I can't believe it. It's actually Mosley. Mosley!" Jessie squealed.

"Hey, birdman, what's up?" Tad said cheerfully.

Jessie wrapped her arms around Mosley. Hollis, Tad, and Livy crowded around. Mosley pointed to the entrance. "I'm delighted to see everyone. Please come with me. I have a surprise for you. Follow me."

Mosley set the group in motion. He gathered everyone outside the front door, then requested silence, and for a moment, they were under his spell. Then Hollis said, "What are we listening for?" Mosley looked at his watch and put his finger to his mouth. In the distance, they could hear a jingling of bells and soon could make out two familiar figures bundled up in the one-horse open sleigh. The closer the sleigh, the happier Livy started to feel. His heart knew before his eyes.

"Oh my, that's Valentine and Anne Rogers," Jessie said.

As the sleigh glided to a halt, Tad called out, "Valentine, I'm not sure if I should hug or strangle you."

Valentine smiled, "Believe me, I know, Tad."

"Beano knew all along that you were alive," Livy said.

Valentine looked at Jessie and Livy in their radiance. "I'm well informed enough to know that congratulations are in order."

"Your uncle is so proud of you, Livy. We're so happy about your news," Anne said admiringly.

As they stepped out of the sleigh and into the foyer, Valentine's and Anne's presence brought a hush to Crumwold Hall. "May I introduce Mr. and Mrs. Valentine Hitch," Mosley announced. The clapping started like a patter of rain and then welled into thunderous applause. Valentine was the common thread. He was on a first-name basis with many of the people in the room. Even before Obie's *come-to-Jesus* moment, Valentine had made his neighbors realize that there was something wrong with where their houses had been built.

"I always knew you were immortal, but I have to say, the ashes thing made me wonder. Those gold sparklers were a surprise," Livy whispered into Valentine's ear.

"It was the remains of that gilded eagle over the mantle in the dining room."

"The sparkles and the weight should have given it away, but I only figured it out yesterday."

"I had to appear to be gone for good. Those photographs I took put everyone I loved in danger."

Anne grabbed Valentine's arm and pulled him closer. "Don't worry, the good guys won."

"I must say, standing in this hall again with you feels really good," Valentine said, giving Anne a kiss.

Livy pulled Tad aside. "Are we set for opening day?"

"Valentine brought the snow. The lift will open around nine. Aldo will be there with his snowmobile, and he'll shuttle everyone to the mountain. "Do you think Valentine will ski?"

"Take a look at him. He's gotten younger," Livy said.

"You can thank Anne."

"I bet you a dollar he skis," Livy said.

Every New Year, at the stroke of midnight, Colonel Rogers would stand up on a chair and call in and bless the future. Then each guest would follow suit. Valentine had already placed the chair over by the fireplace, and as midnight approached, the music came to a stop, and Valentine helped Anne climb onto the chair.

Her toast shattered eighty years of solitude. "Hello everyone, I'm Anne Rogers, the colonel's great-granddaughter. This house has always held a special place in my imagination. I never lived here, but I happened to meet my husband Valentine sneaking in for my first look around while he was sneaking in for a picture. Talk about double jeopardy. If you had told me that day that we would be standing here, I would have thought you were off your rocker. My great-grandfather was the fifth Archibald Rogers to have lived in Crum Elbow, and everyone thought our story ended with his death. My family has been living in the fantasy of this house for generations. Mr. Obermeyer after several generations picked up where the last Archibald Rogers left off. Mr. Obermeyer is not well. I'd like to pray for our liberator."

After a moment of silence, Anne called out, "To our protector."

The applause grew louder.

"To Rupert Obermeyer. To Obie."

The crowd burst into: For he's a jolly good fellow, who nobody can deny."

Valentine helped Anne step down, declined the chair, and then launched into a flow of gratitude. "When I left Crum Elbow, I went from terror into the arms of my darling Anne. I left because of a threat, not only to my life, but to my Burleighwood family. I never expected to return. I realize faking my death was a little extreme, but death threats to my family left me no choice. I'd like to toast my nephew Livingston Hitch. Livy was the end of the line. It would have been very easy for him to go back to California, but he answered the call, and here we are."

After a few moments, Livy jumped on the chair and raised his glass. "Thank you, Valentine. There's someone else who needs to be thanked, a special person, Obie's eyes and ears, Emmett Stone, our resident hydrologist, the voice of the river. Here's to Emmett's big, bright light. May it always light the way." Livy said.

Emmett replaced Livy on the chair and raised his glass to Livy. "To a simple twist of fate. Livy picked me up hitchhiking in Silver Plume, Colorado, and brought me all the way here, and by some wondrous coincidence, Obie picked me up along the side of Route 9 and the rest is history. It was only by collaborating with a man of means that we got this far. We never could have accomplished this by petitioning local officials. Obie was first and foremost a businessman. He believed that if we turned the historic bend at Crum Elbow into a National Park, proclaimed Crumwold Hall an Historic Landmark, and also kept the franchises out, local business would thrive from tourism. Of course, even with all the money in the world, it still comes down to the will of Crum Elbow's citizens. At Obie's behest, a fair number of you in this great hall have made the decision to move your house to the new neighborhood, and by 2045, Crum Elbow's land reclamation will be completed."

The hall erupted in one big smile.

"The Crumwold Foundation plans to turn this great Hall into a cultural seed bank," Emmett continued. "Obie has discretely provided the funds to create a safety net and provide opportunity to the youth in the Hudson Valley who otherwise might easily get lost. Obie was particularly interested in tapping into the gold mine of unrealized talent in the inner city of our neighbor to the south, Poughkeepsie. He wants to try the idea of busing for intellectual equality. I won't go into the details of this vast alternative education project. Obie's mission is to help underachievers find their North Star before hopelessness sets in. Just as somebody gave Obie a hand up out of difficult circumstances, now he's putting his hand forward. So, let's be on with it."

Looking like a local statue of liberty, Jessie raised her champagne glass high. "I'm so glad you're all here. We're off to a great start. Thank you for showing up tonight to ring in the future. We're particularly thankful to those who have sold their houses, moved on, and are still here tonight feeling a strong sense of satisfaction. I think the Colonel would be proud," she raised her glass and took a tiny sip.

Hollis followed with his toast from on high. "It's so nice to be on the winning side of the revolution for a change. Here's to being alive to tell the tale."

Then all attention turned to Tad, who struggled briefly to find his balance on the chair. With duty, honor, country, and Marine confidence, he raised his glass. "To Jessie. She found the John Singer Sargent painting that got Burleighwood out of debt. She brought the farm back, and she got Livy to grow up," he said, winking at Livy. "It took him a little time, but he came around, with a little help from vampires and cows. Here's to Jessie and Livy," Tad said, finishing off his bubbly in one gulp.

As person after person stepped up and offered their toast to the future, Valentine and Anne snuck away on their awaiting sleigh into the snow-lit night.

CHAPTER 23

I spent my lifetime making the invisible visible, as you see.

—Valentine Hitch, *Crook's Paradise*

Overnight, a foot of light, dry powder had blanketed the heavenly Valley. They had gone to bed in the middle of a snowstorm and happily awakened to find the storm clouds scattered and warm morning sunlight pouring through the sky light. Jessie slipped out of bed, leaving Livy to fend for his hangover. She grabbed her Black Diamond back-county skis, poles, and climbing skins. She tied her hair in a ponytail, put on her ski helmet and goggles, and crunched down the porch steps in her touring boots. Jessie then clicked into her bindings, pulled her goggles down, and set out on the single-track trail with her skis gliding through the snow. This was a perfect storm, and the lake effect of the Hudson had turned the powder into champagne. When she reached the carriage road, there were already ski tracks out to the Spotted Cow.

Someone had beaten her to fresh powder, not surprising since the opening of the ski run, the Spotted Cow, was an important, well-publicized day. For the past four years, after a snowstorm, Jessie had found solitude in early morning visits to the former ski hill. The power was always fresh because it was her secret ski spot. No one even knew about or remembered the Spotted Cow.

When she arrived at the top of the mile-long slope, Jessie looked down the mountain, across the railroad tracks, and the frozen river. She traversed far over to the left of the hill to her favorite launching pad, which was technically out of bounds. Jessie, preparing to drop off an eight-foot cliff, gazed out at the deep, azure sky and pulled her goggles down. Then, she took the plunge without a second thought. She was airborne for a second, then stuck the landing in the welcoming powder. Thought-free, she descended the fall line before arcing into wide, round-turns, summoning up a rooster tail of snow in exhilaration.

One of the new schoolers at the base had spotted Jessie in the air and stopped to watch the rest of her run. As she side-slipped to a stop at the bottom, the teenager called out, "Nice skiing, Jessie. You can hit one of our kickers anytime. We're working on one for the railroad tracks. Tanner plans to launch over the Ethan Allen Amtrak Express, as it heads down from Albany."

Jessie laughed."How's the landing?"

"It's steep, but don't go too big or you'll land on flat ice."

Jessie put her skins on and started the trek back up the hill. She got in two more runs in before Tad showed up to open the lift. Tad had charmed a customer out of a snowmobile and came around the blind corner with Valentine clinging to the back and his skis. Following closely behind, Aldo dropped off Livy and headed back down the mountain to fetch the non-skiers, Hollis and Anne. At the bottom, Tad fired up the massive fieldstone fireplace that predated even the rope tow.

Tad cranked the repurposed tractor engine he'd rigged, and the rope tow came to life. The Spotted Cow was back in operation. Valentine stepped into his skis and grabbed the rope. Jessie waited for Livy, and they followed Valentine up the lift, admiring his wolfskin ski jacket and aviator glasses. His Kneissl White Star skis were from 1972. Although beloved by The Beatles and James Bond, Valentine's overly tall, clumsy skis were now better suited for decoration above a fireplace.

At the top of the hill, Valentine buckled his ski boots. So far so good. His ski poles were left over from an earlier era. The baskets were the size of a child's snowshoe. Valentine had always skied the edges of time.

Livy and Jessie joined Valentine at the top and adjusted their boots. Livy was a real product of the eighties with his bright green CB ski jacket and orange Olin Mark IV twin tips. Jessie was the kind of skier everyone took note of because she was usually the best skier on the mountain.

"Let's give it up to gravity," Valentine called out.

"Go for it, Valentine," Livy said.

"We have your back," Jessie assured him.

Valentine smiled and started off in a wedge, slowly plowing through the snow, with Jessie and Livy close behind him in a *slow plow*. It took a while for Valentine to traverse the steeper part of the hill. He found his mojo, slapped his tails together, planted his pole, and aimed his ski tips downhill. With a sudden gust of gravity, Valentine lost his balance and leaned over like a half-dead tree, but at the last second, he recovered and continued down the hill. He was pleased to see Anne and Hollis at the bottom, warming their hands by the fire. He skied over to join them for a hot chocolate.

Livy and Jessie skied over to Valentine. "I guess one run was all you needed."

Valentine nodded. "Yes, it's more about symbolism than my athleticism."

The next run, Livy and Jessie carved joyful figure eights into the snow. At the bottom, Jessie continued on toward the railroad tracks at high speed. Livy followed close behind, until he realized Jessie was heading straight for the big jump. Jessie came down the in-run, and with a remarkable display of flotation, sailed over the railroad bed and disappeared from sight. Livy had veered off to the EZ pass-jump, which cleared the tracks by a foot. Remerging with a long glide across the ice, Jessie and Livy both came to a stop, turned around, and looked back up the hill at Valentine with his poles raised above his head in triumph. With that, a red-tailed hawk launched victoriously from a branch over Charles Crook's Paradise.

ACKNOWLEDGEMENTS

Through revision after revision, Sudama Mark Kennedy acted as my sounding board. Our back-and-forth exchanges helped reshape the story into the novel it is today.

This book would have not happened without the understanding and encouragement of my loving wife Elizabeth and the tremendous inspiration of my son Spencer.

ABOUT DAVID MANDY

David Mandy is from apple country: the Hudson Valley, specifically Highland, New York. He began his journey as an undiagnosed dyslexic and found his voice as a poet. His earliest and most enduring literary influence was Washington Irving.

After studying English and American Literature in graduate school at New York University, he landed a job as a copywriter in Manhattan. He developed an ear for culture working on such clients as Coca-Cola, Alka-Seltzer and Garfield Fruit Snacks.

The same Hudson Valley that gave us Rip Van Winkle also inspired in David *Crook's Paradise*. There's no substitute for steady persistence and belief in oneself. Eventually the forces of destiny prevail.

TO MY READERS

If you loved this story, *Crook's Paradise,* please write a telling review on Amazon.

—David Mandy

R. R. STATION

CRUMWOLD

F. W. VANDERBILT
MANSION

TOWN HALL

JAMES
ROOSEVELT
LIBRARY

HYDE
PARK

ROUTE 9

ELEMENTARY
SCHOOL

POST
OFFICE

ST. JAMES
CHURCH

SITE
OF
FIRST
BARD
HOUSE

NEWBOLD
HOUSE

TWO 18th CENTURY
DUTCH HOUSES

ST. JAMES CHAPEL

EAST PARK ROAD

DICKINSON MILL

EAST
PARK

CRUM ELBOW CREEK

BENJAMIN
HAVILAND
FARM

SITE OF
UNION CORNERS
RACE TRACK

FRANKLIN D. ROOSEVELT
HIGH SCHOOL

VAL-KILL
FARMS

PICTORIAL MAP
of
HYDE PARK

From Rosedale to St. James Church is
3.3 miles. From the Franklin D. Roosevelt
Library to Top Cottage is 3 miles.

www.ingramcontent.com/pod-product-compliance
Lightning Source LLC
Chambersburg PA
CBHW022152240626
47153CB00007B/2625